CHANGING TIMES

By

KayCee Galivan

PROLOGUE

Willow caught movement out of the corner of her eye amidst the grey-blue chop of the ocean surface. She was standing on the deck of the dive boat attached to the *Learn of the Sea*, which was an educational vessel attached to a renowned American university. Turning her attention in the direction of the movement, she watched the surface of the waves as they gently rolled under her feet.

There. She saw it again. A grey fin was slicing through the water. It didn't have the bobbing action of dolphins. Suddenly, Willow's heart was in her throat as she keyed the radio, "We've got a shark at the surface."

Scanning around, she saw another fin, and then a third. "Make that sharks. They seem to be circling around the boat," she reported.

Willow's throat tightened and fear for the divers under the boat caused her heart to start hammering against her ribs. She recognized this as the moment she had been sent here for and she needed to think quickly. Her mind was whirling with possible options to rescue Professor Zach Tyler and the rest of the divers. Some of them were students with limited diving experience. While she wanted everyone back in the boat safely, Zach was her priority. But she was feeling helpless as hundreds of feet of water as well as the dangerous sharks separated her from the man she was supposed to be protecting. All her effort to get herself into this position would be for naught if she failed in her mission now.

CHAPTER ONE

2172, Time Enforcement Patrol home base, New Panama

Colonel Bishop Keene was seated at his desk at TEP headquarters which consisted of barracks and training grounds for new recruits, indoor training and simulation labs for TEP operatives, and the administrative offices where he was located. He had just been given a mission from the Time Tribunal for one of his officers. It was up to him to decide the best person on his team for the assignment. When time travel had been discovered, the leaders of the world's cities had elected a Time Tribunal who, in turn, had created the Time Enforcement Patrol or TEP.

He was the leader of the group of elite officers who would travel back in time on missions that the Tribunal, with guidance from the Artificial Intelligence computer system, determined to be of low risk relative to the value that would be added to improve Earth's present situation. The AIs had also been tasked with trying to figure out ways to erase major historical events that could positively impact life in their present. The officers of TEP were responsible for both preserving history and working to nudge it in little ways that would improve humanity's way of life now.

TEP officers had been sanctioned to use whatever force necessary to meet their mission goals. Consequently, they were sometimes assassins and sometimes babysitters. Other times they were thieves. They also had a role in their present to guard the technology of time travel so that no one tried to go back to the past for their own purposes or financial gain. Unsanctioned time travel was strictly forbidden and severely punished.

Although it was tempting to many to go back in time and make a big change such as assassinating a political leader with the blood of millions on their hands, the AIs had determined that the consequences of such a major change to history would have consequences that would be impossible to predict. Someone even worse could rise to power in the vacuum created.

Bishop was one of the few people who had dual memories of how dire the situation had been for the human race. He could remember a time when the planet had been devoid of vegetation and the Pacific Ocean had been a radioactive toxic mess. However, a couple of years ago, simultaneous missions conducted by people on his team, had been successful in saving the birds and preventing the catastrophe that had caused the environmental damage to the massive Pacific Ocean.

However, the Earth, and the human race, were still struggling. There had been a cataclysmic climate change in 2043 when the effects of a red giant star going supernova hundreds of years before had finally reached Earth. At first, people thought it was kind of cool that there were now two suns. However, the different position of the new sun in the sky led to more hours of daylight which had increased the temperature of the Earth. The crops had failed, and oceans had risen.

The drastic changes in weather had led to massive famine and collapse of governments. Fresh water became difficult to find. Millions had died from diseases and famine. Then, because light travels faster than matter, in 2050, the blast wave from the explosion of the giant star had hit the Earth and the radiation had created even more damage.

Some of the world's leaders of the time had been concerned about that possibility early on and positioned a linked group of supercomputers that had developed into their Artificial Intelligence network and housed them in specially designed bunkers deep below the surface of the Earth. That move had protected the computers from the electromagnetic pulse wave that had swept over the surface of the Earth. It had wiped out the power grid and many of the other infrastructures that supported twenty-first century life.

The Artificial Intelligence computer network had helped the human race survive. The new leaders of the world had been able to input scenarios and get advice about the plans that would have the greatest likelihood of success. They had identified the areas around the world that would likely be flooded by rising ocean levels as the polar and glacial ice melted. Nuclear reactors were decommissioned, and the core reactor materials were buried deep underground. Some of the coastal city inhabitants had relocated to higher ground but others had insisted on staying, thinking that sandbags and earthen berms would save their cities. However, the cyclones and hurricanes had become more intense as the oceans warmed. The pounding waves and high surf had wiped out the efforts to hold back the water, flooding many major cities.

Humans had been forced to basically start over. The traditional motor vehicles of the twenty-first century had been abandoned as humans couldn't afford the production costs of the fossil fuels needed to run them. The materials consumed to extract and refine the crude oil was no longer cost effective. Wind, solar and hydropower were the sustainable sources of power humans had to rely on. Everything else consumed too many of their scarce resources to be worth the effort.

The nuclear facilities that had had not already been shut down had gone into meltdown when the computers that regulated them failed after being wiped out by the EMP. This had left nuclear hotspots in certain areas that still had to be avoided. Toxic waste had also polluted the water in many areas so there were limited places where human habitation was possible. Small enclaves around the world had survived and retained the technological advances made in the early twenty-first century.

The remaining cities had constructed buildings of stone and mortar that would be able to withstand the harsher elements. With the trees gone in many places, the winds had little to impede their progress and dunes formed and reformed with the massive dust storms that developed regularly.

There were some seed banks that had saved plant diversity and they had managed to construct some biodomes that helped protect the remaining plants from the elements and allowed people to grow the foods needed to sustain life. However, the global population was expanding and there was now concern that the cities would be unable to keep up with the demand before long. Many residents of the various settlements tended their food plots under the domes as their full-time jobs. Each family would have to contribute some of their produce to the people like TEP officers and the Civil Defense officers who had the job of protecting the settlements.

There were also some domestic animals that humans had been able to save. Their numbers were small due to the resources they consumed but much of the wild biodiversity of the planet had been lost. One might logically think that the life in the sea would have escaped the ravages of these changes. However, when the oceans had risen, the contents of many landfills had been washed out to sea. The plastic materials had been broken down by the sunlight and microplastic debris consumed by the marine life killed off some species and made most of the rest unsafe for humans to consume.

For individuals who could afford them or those, like TEP agents, who needed them for their work, solar-powered hovercrafts were the major mode of transportation. The vehicle was ideal for traveling over the sandy landscape. The traditional motor vehicles of the twenty-first century had been abandoned as they couldn't navigate the terrain and the fossil fuels needed to run them weren't cost effective. The hovercraft could travel at speeds over 160 kilometers per hour in ideal conditions.

The remaining settlements had been established close to the equator since that zone allowed for maximum growing seasons and required less energy to keep the inhabitants warm in the winter months. Transit between the cities was conducted by larger, high-speed hydrofoil boats that could make the trip across the Atlantic in half a day. The trip across the Pacific was longer and that vessel usually had sleeping berths for the day-long trip.

Commander Bishop Keene also recruited and trained new officers when there was a position open. His people had to have a lot of knowledge of history and language skills. Obviously, no one officer would be able to know everything or speak every language, so they had developed specialists. Regions of the world were divided, and officers learned the history and languages of that area. While a TEP operative didn't have to be fluent, they had to have passable language skills. There had been consideration given to developing implanted linguistic chips that would interface with an officer's speech and language centers in their brains. While the technology would have provided certain advantages, ultimately the idea was rejected. The concern was raised that the chip would be difficult to retrieve if an agent died on assignment. No one wanted to risk having such advanced technology falling into the wrong hands. Such a development could, in its own way, alter historical events in unpredictable ways.

As Bishop considered the best operative on his team for this new assignment, he considered the strengths and expertise of each person. He knew where and when each of his people were and who was currently available. Looking at the details of the assignment, he knew exactly which agent would be perfect for this job.

CHAPTER TWO

Willow Randall had completed her last time jump several days ago and she hated sitting around waiting for her next assignment. She had traveled back to the near-past, to 2018, on an errand to retrieve some files that contained dark-web chatter that had been lost with the EMP burst. The AIs were constantly being fed new material by programmers so that their information database continued to expand. Occasionally, as with her last mission, some seemingly random fact prompted the computers to request more data to complete a bigger picture.

Like all TEP officers returning from each mission, she had undergone a decontamination process that involved showers and ultraviolet light treatments. Every agent's least favorite part of the decon was the respiratory cleanse. Because the population of Earth was smaller and immunity to certain diseases may have been lost, world leaders didn't want to risk bringing something back from the past such as the Plague that could wipe out the humans left. Pathogens could be harbored internally, and quarantining for several weeks wasn't an efficient use of personnel. So, before authorizing time travel, the Tribunal had mandated the establishment of effective methods to cleanse the travelers before reintroducing them to the community. The respiratory process involved inhaling a special combination of gases and chemicals that purged the sinuses and lungs of the time traveler. There was oxygen in the mix so that one didn't pass out. However, the chemicals irritated the lungs and people always seemed to cough for a few hours afterward.

Willow loved the water so, to help pass her downtime, she headed for the training pool. After swimming some laps, she pushed herself through the underwater obstacle course. Then, she cooled down by swimming some backstroke laps, enjoying the flow of the water over and around her body as she cut smoothly through it. She figured that she would work on her monthly psych competencies once she was back in uniform.

Every TEP operative worried something that had occurred during their mission would have ripple changes into the present they returned to. The computers calculated for the mission agenda but agents always worried that something unforeseen could result in something as drastic as preventing themselves or someone they knew from being born. People could really drive themselves crazy contemplating the effects of their actions on the timeline. It had been too much for some of the earlier field agents as the fear could paralyze an operative when they needed to make split-second decisions. Field agents underwent a lot of simulations in their training to help them develop their skills and deal with their doubts.

Willow was saved from those exercises though. When she emerged from the pool, she saw that Commander Keene had summoned her to his office and she hoped that meant he had an assignment for her. She was eager to hear what he had to say so she messaged that she had been training in the pool and would report as quickly as she could.

In record time, she was in uniform and standing in front of headquarters, scanning her invisible biometric tattoo in her wrist for admittance. Willow was taller than average with a lithe build. She had fine, straight, pale blonde hair that she wore long. It fell past her shoulders down to the middle of her back. When in uniform, she wore it in a tidy braid. Her bright blue eyes were set in a delicate face with a tanned complexion. She looked like she could have just as easily walked down a catwalk in Paris or off the beach in southern California.

When Commander Keene's door opened for her to be admitted, she went in and took a seat across the desk from her boss. He welcomed her and got right to the point, as he typically did, "Randall, you did well on your last assignment. For the sake of continuity, I think that you would be a good fit for this next one. The information you collected has been fed into the AIs and they have reached an important conclusion. That is what has prompted this next mission."

Willow knew that any response at this point was unnecessary, so she continued listening as Bishop went on speaking, "There was a marine biologist working on the Earth's problem with microplastics polluting the waters in 2018. His name was Zachary Tyler and he had claimed to have a breakthrough by discovering a process that would scrub those particles out of seawater. As you know, our oceans were so contaminated that the fish have been inedible for decades and, only recently, was a solution to the problem found. The computers feel that the professor's process would waste fewer resources and have greater benefit."

Willow was unfamiliar with the scientist and his work but recognized that if someone could have impacted the issue many years sooner, the ocean would have been able to provide sustainable resources for many more of the remaining inhabitants of Earth, so she nodded.

Bishop went on, "Professor Tyler had evidently been approached by a large petrochemical company about purchasing the breakthrough, but the scientist refused their offer. I personally find it laudable that he had stated publicly that he was going to give it away for free because the issue was more important than money."

Willow was surprised by that statement. To walk away from a potential multi-million-dollar deal and give the technology away was virtually unheard of. Silently, she figured that either he was a man to be admired or he hadn't really worked out the process yet.

"Now, this is where the story really gets interesting and the AIs want you to come in," Bishop kept talking, "Before Tyler could publish his work, he was killed in a diving accident while at sea on his research vessel. He apparently took everything about the process with him when he died."

Willow felt a wave of disappointment and said, "Wow, that's really bad luck."

Bishop's expression was grim as he replied, "That leads me to the information you retrieved on your last mission. Apparently, the professor's death wasn't really an accident. An unknown entity on the dark web contracted with an unidentified member of the boat's crew to kill Tyler and make it look like an accident. Also, his computer was to be destroyed so that all traces of the breakthrough process would be lost. We don't know if he really died in an accident or if it was intentional sabotage."

Willow grew angry as she listened. To think that a way to save the world's oceans had been snuffed out seemed senseless.

Bishop had finished the back story and got to the point, "Your mission will be to travel back to 2018 and protect Professor Tyler. The AIs calculate that having our oceans cleaner decades earlier will have tremendous benefits for the inhabitants of Earth now."

Willow was eager for the assignment, "Yes, Sir!"

"I'll forward all the mission specs to you. Report to the Armory to prepare. You will make your jump tomorrow."

Knowing that their meeting was concluded, Willow rose as she said, "Thank you, Sir," and left. Her eagerness for an assignment was strengthened by the objective of this mission. The opportunity to improve the health of the planet was something she took very seriously.

CHAPTER THREE

Willow had made her requisitions with the Armory
and was now in the Archives reading all the material they
had about her assignment, Zachary Tyler. As Commander
Keene had said, the marine biologist had seemed to be on
the verge of a breakthrough. When she pulled up his picture,
Willow was surprised that Zachary Tyler appeared to be
much younger than she thought a university professor would
typically be. He was also far more good-looking than she had
expected, not that Willow had really paused to consider the
question when she had begun her research.

Zachary had a finely chiseled face with a wide, genuine
smile and even teeth. The hint of dimples were visible in his
cheeks. His grey eyes were framed with glasses, which added
a studious quality to his appearance. His dark brown hair was
worn short and combed to one side. His information had him
listed as six foot one in height and he appeared to be fit and
muscular without being overweight. That was, again, not
what Willow would have expected. She would have thought
that a scientist spent all his time researching things and not

working out. She couldn't help the unexpected thought that this assignment might end up being even more interesting than she had anticipated.

The next day, she collected her gear and headed her speeder to the ruins of Washington, District of Columbia. It had been the capital of the United States at the time that she was heading back to. The costal elements of the terrain had caused the whole city to be under water when the ocean levels had been at their highest. The area was still prone to flooding and storm surges, but it wasn't prone to the dune formations that plagued other parts of the continent.

She hoped that the location she wanted to use for her jump would be a viable option. It would save her a lot of time and twenty-first century money if she could time travel in a location near Virginia Beach. That was where the professor's boat would soon be departing from. Certainly, no one planning the voyage would expect that the leader of the expedition wouldn't be returning. Willow resolved that, with her intervention, Zachary Tyler would complete his research and return to Virginia Beach alive at the completion of the trip.

When she drew near to the ruins of the city, she could make out the broken dome of what had once been the Capital Building. The uneven white edges stood out against the bright blue of the sky. The chaos that had filled this city during the years of upheaval still felt like a heavy shroud hanging over the place. Passing through the heart of the city was like travelling down a deserted canyon. Willow felt very small and alone in what had once been a thriving city. A layer of sand covered the pavement where the city streets had been. The taller buildings had a water line on them marking the point where they had once been partially submerged.

When she turned a corner, she could see the location she sought looming at the end of the street. It was a box-like structure that took up the entire block. She hoped that she could find a way into Nationals Stadium from the street level because she really didn't want to have to climb the sheer wall in front of her. Willow navigated her craft slowly around the massive structure, scanning the entryways that had been barricaded with bars and wood for any gap in them.

When she spotted a dark shadow, she came to a stop. After parking and arming the antitheft feature on her speeder, she grabbed her gear and hopped out. As she drew close to the break in the wood panel that had been secured over an entrance, she could see that the hole would be big enough for her to squeeze through. She really hoped that she wouldn't find any rats when she poked her head inside. She really hated rats. Despite all the climate and habitat changes, the rodents were one of the few animals that had managed to survive. However, they were riddled with diseases and being bitten by one was dangerous.

When Willow made sure that her entry point was safe, she slipped inside the stadium. The area underneath the seating of the stadium was dark and she used the time while her eyes were completely adjusting to settle her backpack over her shoulders. Following the light streaming from the top of the concrete stairs, she began climbing. There were obviously more direct routes to her destination, but she didn't want to risk getting lost in the service tunnels under the stands. Figuring that the climb would be good exercise for the day, she set off at a brisk pace.

When she reached the top of the stairs, the expanse of the stadium became visible. The metal of the seats had been ripped out and melted down for another use a long time ago, leaving a wide expanse of terraced concrete. Insects had long ago destroyed the field where baseball had been played, leaving only barren dirt.

In the middle of what had been the infield was the raised area that had been the pitcher's mound. Thankfully, the stadium had not been filled in with blowing sand or flood debris and she made her way down to what remained of the playing field. The silence of the place was eerie and although her footfalls were soft, she felt like the sounds of her breaths and steps echoed back at her as she moved. Willow couldn't help the way that the hair on the back of her neck tingled with alarm. Occasionally, she paused in her descent to scan her surroundings. Despite her feelings of anxiety, she seemed to be alone.

At the bottom of the stairs, she hopped over the low wall and onto the dirt of the playing field. Willow had already programmed her belt for a date when the AIs had indicated that the team had not been playing ball. As an extra precaution, even though it was midday now, she would be jumping into the darkest time of early morning. She just had to press one button to prime the equipment. She trotted over to what had been the pitcher's mound and, as she reached the top of the gentle rise, she elbowed the second button and disappeared.

Summer, 2018, Washington, District of Columbia, United States

Willow was standing on the pitcher's mound which was now surrounded by green grass, visible in the moonlight. It was 0300 and she hoped that any security patrolling the stadium wouldn't notice her. Still, she didn't want to linger, so she sprinted back to the stands which were now filled with organized rows of seats. She had never used this jump point but, so far, it was looking like it had been a good choice.

Quickly climbing the stairs away from the field, Willow paused once she was again in the shadows of the entryway that would take her back to street level. Glancing down into the gloom, she could now make out a glowing red EXIT sign. Willow could hear the measured sound of footsteps echoing up from the concourse below her. Quickly she melted back into the shadows and flattened herself against the wall at her back. Although the guard would be unlikely to hear her, she forced her breathing to a slower, shallower pattern, despite her recent exertion.

Moments later, the beam of a flashlight pierced the darkness at the base of the stairs. Then the guard's portly dark form appeared in the periphery of the light. His cadence didn't faulter and he never glanced her way as he passed the opening and continued on his route. Willow listened for another moment as the footfalls continued to fade before she crept the rest of the way down the stairs. Arriving at the bottom, she carefully peeked out in the direction the guard had come from in case they patrolled at intervals. Seeing no one, she then shifted her gaze to the retreating form of the guard who had just passed. Since his back was to her and he seemed oblivious to her presence, she scoped out the exit to the street directly across from her. There was a retractable scissor divider which was likely locked, flanked by twin trash receptacles.

Willow scampered in a crouch across the concourse until she was concealed by the trash bins. Then, she pulled out her lock picks. All TEP agents were trained to get out of secured situations and most carried a set of picks with them on missions, though they were often concealed in gear more appropriate to the period they were travelling to. Because this was a near-time trip, Willow was able to carry a deluxe set. She made short work of the lock. With another peek in both directions, she determined there wasn't a guard nearby. As quietly as she could, she slid the gate just wide enough to slip through before closing it behind her with a secure click.

Next, she turned her attention to the metal door that was her last barrier before she would be on the street. It was jointed metal on roller tracks and would have to be lifted from the bottom. There was also a lock on the handle that would have to be picked before she could lift it. She looked around in the shadows but there wasn't anything she would be able to prop the door up with while she slid under it. With a mental shrug, she went to work on the second lock. When it was free, she removed her backpack, laid down on the concrete, and lifted the door. After sliding her bag through, she had no problem holding the door up enough to wriggle underneath it.

Once outside, the streetlights were much brighter than the interior of the stadium. After a quick look up and down the street, Willow slid the rest of the way from under the door. Then she raised it enough to retrieve her backpack before she allowed it to settle back to the floor and stood up. She scooped up her bag and sprinted across the empty pavement and began walking down the sidewalk. The AIs had prepared a list of potential places for her to stay as part of her mission brief, so she made her way the four blocks to her first option.

It was a seedy hotel that appeared to rent rooms by the hour but that was perfect for Willow's needs. She wore jeans and a t-shirt with a rounded neckline, so she pulled up the cotton of the shirt and tied it in a quick knot through the neck of the shirt. The move bared her midriff and exposed the swell of each breast. She quickly worked her bra off and out from under the t-shirt. The night air through the thin cotton caused her nipples to bead up, making them plainly visible under the fabric. Then she pulled the low-rise jeans down a bit lower on her hips. It wasn't a great hooker look, but passable.

The desk clerk of the motel had a bored expression, but he perked up when he saw Willow walk in.

In an effort to appear like the usual clientele, she said as she approached the window, "Got a room tonight? I got a guy coming in a few minutes."

The rates were posted on a torn piece of paper that had been taped haphazardly to the upper corner of the glass separating them and Willow fished out the appropriate bills.

The man handed her a key on a plastic tab with the number 17 on it and Willow continued, "He'll be by himself. He's middle-aged and a little overweight. Will you send him my way when he gets here?"

"Yeah, I can do that," the guy leaned closer to the glass and said, "I haven't seen you around before. Maybe you want to hang around when he's done, and we could have a go?"

Inwardly repulsed by the offer, Willow gave him a big grin and arched a brow, "Sure, why not?"

As she turned away, she swayed her hips with some exaggeration and resolved to leave through the bathroom window to avoid the creep. She only hoped that, now, when her 'john' didn't show up, the man wouldn't be knocking on her door before she was ready to leave.

Once she was in the run-down room, Willow quickly pulled out the computer she had carried with her. It was designed to look appropriate for the time but was more powerful. The programming in it would allow her to hack just about anything. All TEP agents had created social media personas that they could use to help establish their backstory for near-time missions. While she waited for the laptop to come online, she put her bra back on and readjusted her clothes.

Then, Willow's first task was to hack into those social media platforms and modify her posts to reflect what she needed for this assignment.

Next, she went into several sailing charter companies and added herself to the rosters of their employees. Lastly, she went into the records of a dive school and added herself into the list of their graduates. Satisfied, with her progress and worried about the randy desk clerk, she powered everything off and repacked her backpack.

When she stepped into the bathroom, she saw that the tub was filthy but there was a small window in the wall above it. Willow managed to open it wide enough to squeeze through and glanced at the ground below. The alley was covered with trash and the stench hit her nostrils immediately. The drop didn't look to be too far, and she hoped fervently that the trash under her feet wouldn't be too rotten when she landed.

She put one knee over the windowsill and was trying to get her pack through when she heard a knock at the door. Resigned that her time was up, Willow pushed the pack ahead of her and eased over. She hung from the sill for a moment, hoping that the trash would cushion her landing without blowing up all over her.

She managed to keep her feet on the uneven pile and staggered away until she was once again on firm footing. Grabbing her bag and sprinting away, Willow had barely taken three steps when she heard an angry exclamation, "Hey, where you goin'?"

Without looking back, Willow sped up and was soon at the end of the alley. She kept up her pace for a couple more blocks. Since she heard no one following her and saw no one on the street behind her, she settled back to a steady walk. The neighborhood was still not particularly upscale, and she began working on the next phase of her plan.

When Willow spotted a car old enough that it likely didn't contain any GPS tracking device, she made short work of breaking in and bypassing the key ignition. Then, she pulled away from the curb and began working her way out of the city. Once she was on the freeway headed for Virginia Beach without alerting the local police, she breathed a sigh of relief and settled into her drive just as the first hint of dawn began to lighten the eastern sky.

CHAPTER FOUR

Summer, 2018, Virginia Beach, Virginia,

Willow had arrived at the docks of the marina where the University's research vessel, *Learn of the Sea*, was moored. She would have a couple days to figure out how to become part of the crew before the ship headed out to sea on the research voyage that Professor Tyler was in danger of not returning from.

Her first stop was the office of the harbormaster. There was a remote possibility that a crew opening on the ship had yet to be filled. After talking with the crusty old man and learning she wasn't going to be so lucky, she left him her name and contact info in case the situation changed.

Then, she settled in to surveil the crew through a pocket telescope as they prepared for the extended voyage. There were pallets of supplies to be carried on board and everyone milling about looked to be capably doing their job. Exploiting a green member's lack of experience wasn't going to be an option.

That left Willow with two choices. She would have to sabotage someone so that they were injured and unable to work. Or, she would have to try to create some drama on board that would get someone fired. She hated the thought of either plan but figured that the second option would be better than plotting to physically harm someone. There were so many ways that personal injury could go wrong.

Resigned, she headed to a coffee bar. After ordering a chai latte, she found a seat and logged her computer into their network. Willow didn't worry too much about being traced, but this tactic would provide some anonymity. With her hacking program, she considered which crew member she would target. Having been given the names of everyone on the crew by the Archivists, she broke into each person's social media accounts as she decided which person to target.

After some consideration she settled on Bruno Wilson. The guy seemed to have a lot of selfies with bikini-clad women and little else on his feed, so Willow decided she wasn't going to feel too badly about her ruse. She began writing posts on his feed disparaging the commander of the boat, Captain Noah Harvey, and Professor Tyler. To top off her misinformation campaign, she added several comments about looking forward to hooking up with as many of the college co-eds as he could during the trip. By mentioning the captain by name, he should become aware of what she had written. Her target didn't seem to post a lot, so hopefully, Bruno wouldn't see the comments and remove them before the captain could see them and become upset.

As it was becoming evening, she went back to the boat and continued watching. It was possible that the crew would get a shore leave prior to sailing. If a simple chance to trip her target up presented itself, she wanted to be close by to take advantage of it.

She didn't wait for long before the crew piled down the gangway and off the docks to a car parked in the lot. Following them to a nearby bar, Willow watched as they seemed to settle in for an evening of heavy drinking.

Willow took up a seat in a shadowy corner of the bar, trying to avoid the attention of the rowdy group of men. She recognized them all from their social media accounts and Bruno was pounding back shots. Soon he was slurring his words as he shouted for another round. He would definitely be hung over the next morning. Perhaps that fact, in combination with his supposed comments would be enough to get him fired. She considered baring some skin and joining the group. She could subtly encourage the men to fight over her. However, if any of the crew remembered her when she hopefully joined them the next day or two, that could prove awkward aboard the boat.

If her current ploy didn't yield any fruit, she would still have around twelve hours to take more drastic actions. So, Willow watched and waited. An idea struck her, and she went out to the parking lot where their vehicle sat waiting. She took a wad of napkins and stuffed it into the tailpipe. The vehicle would start but stall out when running. Having car trouble would get them back to the boat even later, which would mean less sleep. If Bruno, that would likely increase the captain's ire.

When the crew staggered out to head back to the docks a short time later, sure enough, the car appeared to be malfunctioning. There was a lot of yelling between the various members of the crew. The engine was checked for a problem, but none could be identified. Frustrated, the they took off on foot since the marina was only about a mile away.

In their inebriated state, they had left the car in the aisle of the lot, blocking traffic. Willow sidled over and removed the napkins before following at a discreet distance. The owner of the bar would likely have the vehicle towed by morning. It was probably too much to wish for that this little change to history would result in a sprained ankle or wrist, but the crew was falling-down drunk, so she could hope.

As Willow watched, several men did stagger over a crack in the sidewalk and careen into each other. Bruno stepped off the curb but caught himself on a parked car. Eventually, they all returned to the boat and swayed up the gangway. Hearing nothing more from aboard the boat, Willow used the time to catch a little sleep herself. She settled in behind some bushes that lined the foundation of the harbormaster's hut. While the car she had stolen was still available, she wanted to be able to hear any commotion aboard the ship in the morning.

Dawn came quickly and the marina began humming with activity. However, aboard the *Learn of the Sea*, there was not much happening. As she watched, a tall, trim man wearing glasses with a ruck sack over his shoulder, made his way down the dock. Willow recognized him and watched as he climbed the gangway and stepped aboard the boat before setting his burden down.

He must have called out because, soon, the captain was hurrying to his side. None of the deck crew had yet made an appearance. Willow had worked her way closer and could see the angry expression on the captain's face before he showed Professor Tyler below deck.

Only a few minutes later, the fire alarm on the ship began blaring. Willow hoped it wasn't a real emergency. A short time later, with no smoke appearing, the alarm stopped. Then she saw the crew scramble onto the foredeck, some still in their skivvies. The captain was livid, pacing back and forth and shouting at the crew. Willow would soon know if her efforts would have the desired effect.

The captain appeared to dismiss all but Bruno, the victim of her smear campaign. He took out his phone and appeared to be reading her posts. The man was understandably surprised, and she could see him pleading with Captain Harvey. Willow didn't know how strict the man was about his boat, but she hoped she had done enough to get Bruno removed from the ship. She felt badly about getting the sailor fired and hoped it wouldn't impact his career too badly, provided he really was more interested in his work than the women he met.

When he was finally dismissed, Bruno headed back below deck and the captain lingered at the rail, staring off at the traffic motoring around the marina. Now, all Willow could do was wait.

Several hours later, she watched her target walk off the boat carrying his bag and wearing his civvies. Apparently, the first portion of her plan had worked. Now, she hoped that Captain Harvey contacted the harbormaster rather than past employees or other captain friends with his need to replace a crew member.

Wandering over to the shack at the entrance to the marina, she poked her head inside and said with a bright smile on her face, "Just wanted to check in with you again to see if anyone was needing a deck hand."

The harbormaster looked up from the chart he had in front of him just long enough to say, "Check over at *Learn of the Sea.*"

Happily, she stepped back out as she said, "Thanks! I owe you one."

Not wanting to seem to be in too much of a hurry, Willow walked down the dock to the boat. Standing on the pier next to it, she could see the large size of the vessel. With a fortifying breath, she climbed aboard and asked to speak to the Captain.

When he appeared, Willow launched in, "Captain, I heard from the harbormaster that you are looking for a crew member. I'm looking for a new job and I'd like to talk to you about my experience."

The older man looked up, startled. After a moment, he replied, "Come to the bridge and let's talk."

Once seated, Captain Harvey asked her a series of questions. Willow thought that he seemed pleased with her responses. Eventually, he tossed her a length of rope and said, "Show me your bowline."

Willow knew that he meant for her to tie the knot that was a quick-release way of securing lines that was standard on boats. She had some experience tying one and had been practicing, so she completed the task quickly and smoothly.

As she handed it back to Captain Harvey, he pulled one end and the knot gave as it should. "You're hired," he pronounced. "Get your gear and report to the First Mate for your bunk assignment. There are a couple other women on the crew. so you'll share a cabin with one of them. We will be sailing in eighteen hours so take care of any shore business you need to. There will be limited land contact and no cell service where we are headed. Then report to the bosun for your assignments."

"Aye, Captain," she replied and exited the bridge. With a quick trip back to her stolen vehicle, Willow gathered her gear and returned to the ship. Now, that she was on board, she needed to find a way to get close to the professor and keep an eye on him.

Professor Zach Tyler had unpacked his gear and was inspecting his equipment. There were three decks on the ship. At the rear of the vessel, was the helicopter landing deck where supplies would be delivered, and their dive launch would be tied up. Moving up from that level, there was a middeck. Separating the middeck from the foredeck was a large common area for meals and the bridge. The crew and student cabins would be below these decks. At the rear of the middeck, there were half a dozen tall glass tubes with hoses connected to the top and bottom. This was the heart of Zach's experiment and he eagerly looked it over. Everything appeared to be ready and he was thankful for that.

Zach had arrived a day ahead of his students because he wanted the peace and quiet to prepare his experiment and settle in. He had been conducting classes on this vessel for several years. He knew that many of the young women who signed up were really just looking for a chance to walk around in their bikinis and get a tan to go with an easy grade. He was also used to having them throw themselves at him, but it was always irritating. There were students at the University with a genuine interest in the ocean. Those serious students in the group would be able to help him with his research. The beach bunnies would be in for a surprise when they found out that they would actually have to work to earn their grade. No doubt, when the first supply chopper came out to restock the ship's supplies, the students that really didn't want to learn would be bailing back to the mainland to drop the class.

Zach climbed a fixed ladder and attached a large syringe to a stopcock in the tubing, injecting the green contents into the glass tube. He repeated the process with each one until the green was swirling around in all of them.

Willow was making her way to the aft of the ship and rounded the corner to see a tall man leaning precariously out from a ladder while messing around with the glass tubes arrayed along the far edge of the deck. Her heart jumped into her throat as she realized that the man was her charge. One little slip and, while he wouldn't likely be killed, the professor would definitely have some broken bones. She hurried over to that side of the deck and looked around to see if anyone else from the crew was nearby, but they were alone.

Willow's next concern was whether or not she should make her presence known. She didn't want to startle the professor and cause the very accident she sought to prevent. She decided that she should speak up because she shouldn't know who he was, and he appeared to be messing around with the equipment. It made sense for her to be vigilant and establish herself as a conscientious employee.

Clearing her throat softly, she spoke up, "Excuse me, sir. I hope that you are supposed to be working with this equipment. Would you mind identifying yourself, please?" Her heart began beating a furious tattoo as Professor Tyler whipped his head around and his piercing grey eyes lasered in on her through his glasses. Although she had thought him handsome from his picture, she wasn't prepared for the jolt of attraction that hit her in the stomach.

Zach was struck speechless for a moment as he saw the lithe blonde woman staring up at him. The sun shown on her face and she held a hand above her eyes, shading them so that she wouldn't have to squint as she looked up. She was wearing the uniform of the deck crew, he quickly noted. So, not one of his co-eds, he concluded.

Zach smiled broadly, liking that she was concerned about keeping his project safe. "I'm Professor Tyler. This project in front of you is part of the reason that we are heading out to sea tomorrow. I'm hoping that the equipment you are looking at will provide the solution for removing microplastics from the oceans. It's still in the preliminary stages but I'm hopeful."

Since he had completed inoculating the tubes with his special strain of algae, Zach began climbing down as he was talking. As he finished speaking, his feet landed firmly on the teak deck of the ship. Zach was surprised that the woman in front of him was tall enough that she was no longer looking up. He was a tall man and it wasn't often that he met a woman who was nearly equal to him in height.

"And who might you be?" he asked.

Willow stuck out her hand and introduced herself, using her alias, with a firm handshake, "Willow McGee. I just signed on with the crew. I hadn't heard anything yet about what research was being conducted on board. Your work sounds like an amazing project, Professor. The problem of plastics contaminating the water is a huge concern. I really hope that your work will make a real difference."

Pleased that she shared his interest and concern for the ocean, Zach smiled. She didn't seem aware that she hadn't withdrawn her hand and he liked the warmth of her touch. "I'm not sure what rules Captain Harvey has about crew interactions with research staff and students, but, feel free to call me Zach," he said. While he had worked with the captain on previous voyages, he didn't want to undermine the man's authority.

Willow felt his quiet confidence and noted the smooth way he had climbed down the ladder. It was safe to say that the man was nothing like the nerd she had stereotyped him to be from the photo in the Archives. Reluctantly, she eased her hand away and said, "Well, Zach, it was great meeting you and I'll be excited to see your experiment in action. But I really need to find my boss and get to work. I want to make a good impression on my first day, after all."

As she turned and Zach watched her walk away, he mused that she had definitely made an impression on him. It was certainly unexpected, and he resolved to put the thought aside and focus on his research.

CHAPTER FIVE

The next morning, just as dawn was breaking, Willow and the rest of the deck crew prepared to cast off the mooring lines. The wooden deck hummed under her feet as the powerful engines rumbled to life. The ship was a hybrid with a retractable sail and solar panels to maximize renewable energy sources to power it. However, to navigate the harbor, they would have to use the engines to get out to sea.

As she worked alongside the other members of the crew, Willow reflected on what she knew about their financial situations. None of them seemed desperate for a quick buck and most had been working in the industry for years. Willow speculated that it was more likely that Professor Tyler's killer was one of the students.

That group was somewhat harder to assess. Several had become successful after the ill-fated voyage and Willow wondered if a cash infusion had paved the way for them. A few of the students had gone on to be well-known in the oceanography community, so they were low on her list. There were a couple who never seemed to amount to much. It was possible that those students had squandered the cash infusion if they were the guilty party. There was one student in particular that Willow was suspicious of. She had gone on to work for one of the petrochemical companies that had tried to purchase Zach's process. While the co-ed was the obvious one to keep her eye on, Willow didn't want to focus all her attention on the woman and miss the real criminal.

While the crew was stowing lines and deflating fenders, Zach had assembled his students on the aft deck and was conducting his first class. Several of the young women were wearing skimpy bikinis and were blatantly trying to catch the professor's eye.

Willow couldn't hide her mirth when the constant bouncing of the deck started to have several of them rushing to the rail to heave up their stomach contents. That was not the way to make teacher's pet. She couldn't help wondering how many of them were on an ocean-going vessel for the first time. It was different than motoring around on a ski boat on a reservoir somewhere inland. Those students were in for a rude awakening. Especially since the seas were relatively calm and there wasn't a cloud in the sky.

Once they were free of the traffic in the harbor, the captain had engaged the sail, so the boat was much quieter as it sliced through the waves and Willow took a moment to enjoy the feel of the salty breeze on her face. Her peace was broken as the radio squawked her name. She was directed by the bosun to report to the galley to assist the cook with meal prep. Disappointed, she glanced back at Zach. Willow figured that he would be safe enough in front of everyone. Also, it was probably a good idea to be involved with preparing the meals in case someone tried to slip her charge some poison.

Tomorrow was the day that Zach would be killed, unless she successfully intervened. If she was able to save him,

Willow would have no way of knowing after that when another attack might be coming. She also needed to get herself onto the diving tender the next day. As the bosun was usually the driver, she would have to slip him something to keep him out of commission in the morning.

    With the ship anchored at the prearranged coordinates, early the next morning Zach was eager to get started on several experiments. They were positioned on the edge of the Atlantic Gulfstream, a fast-moving current of water within the ocean. He had started his algae experiment as soon as the anchor had caught last night. His process worked by pumping seawater into the top of each of the glass tubes at a set flow rate. His specially engineered algae then ate the microplastics in the water before it was released from the bottom of the tube back into the ocean. Each tube had been set to a different flow rate and had an inline filter to catch residual plastics, thereby helping him establish the optimal rate that his algae could process the water. The filter also kept the algae from being released with the seawater. Zach was hopeful that the sunshine would help the microbes multiply and function more efficiently. After several days, he hoped to see crude oil collecting at the top of the tube where it would be siphoned off and the amount would be recorded. The crude oil was formed as a waste product as the algae digested the microplastics. He hoped, later on in the experiment, to see how coarsely ground the plastics could be while still allowing his algae to break them down.

    The purpose of the day's dive was to collect water samples from various depths around the vessel. The students with little dive training would be collecting where there wasn't as much current to contend with. He and several other seasoned divers would be doing the trickier work of collecting samples from within the Gulfstream. It was Zach's theory that, because the current was picking up more plastics from the shore of the United States and the water was more turbulent, the concentration of microplastics would be higher in the faster moving current. If this proved to be the case, he hoped that positioning his equipment within the faster current would compound the benefit of the water the algae cleaned.

Willow had been up early and slipped a mild medication into the bosun's breakfast that was designed to relieve constipation. She hoped that she had given him enough to keep him in the bathroom for the morning. But she hated to see the man suffering from diarrhea too long. Awaiting the rest of the team's waking and preparing for the day, she took the opportunity to check all the dive equipment thoroughly. There were no loose hoses and every tank was filled. She marked one of the tanks and bled off the oxygen before refilling it from the gas generator on board. Willow then taped over the release valve so that she could see if anyone had tampered with it after her efforts. She wanted to be sure that the gas Zach would be breathing was indeed oxygen and not nitrogen. The tank could look full but if it was the wrong gas, the result would be deadly. Since deep dives would use a combination of gases, both were available at the filling station and it would be an easy way to sabotage the professor without anyone knowing.

As the students and deck crew began to assemble on the aft deck a short time later, the co-eds were divided into two groups. Some were assigned experiments on the boat and others were instructed to don their dive gear.

Willow had been surprised by Zach's appearance on deck. Gone were the glasses and his fit body was clad in swim trunks that came partway down his tan, muscled thigh. Stretched across his torso and defining his pecs was a matching yellow long-sleeved rash-guard shirt. While there wasn't any coral to be concerned about, the material would also filter the bright sunlight and offer some protection against burning. His hair was blowing around in the wind on deck and Willow could see golden glints that indicated he was no stranger to sunshine. The overall effect caused her stomach to flutter a little and she resolved to put thoughts about how luscious his body was firmly out of her head. However, despite her best effort, Willow couldn't decide which version of the man was sexier, the studious professor or the buff diver.

A call came over the shipboard radios and broke into Willow's musings. It was from the bosun stating that he was going to be too ill to pilot the dive boat.

Quickly keying her radio, Willow responded, "I could step in, Captain Harvey. I have diving experience."

She waited with bated breath as the radio was silent. This part of her plan was the biggest gamble. If she didn't get on the dive boat, she would have to wait in agony on the ship, wondering if Zach was going to return and if her efforts so far would be enough to save the man's life. Then, relief flowed through her as she heard the Captain say, "Okay. Willow, you'll take his place."

"Aye, Captain," she replied, trying to hide her eagerness.

Zach had a few more instructions for the students diving with him and Willow took the opportunity to check the tanks one last time. The marked tank didn't appear to have been tampered with. However, there was another tank that had the needle on the gauge now registering close to the red zone, indicating that most of the air had been removed. Quickly refilling it, Willow surreptitiously watched the co-eds to see if any of them were paying attention to what she was doing, but no one seemed to care.

One of the girls going on the dive was dressed in another skimpy bikini and seemed determined to catch Zach's eye. He told them to grab their gear and reconvene at the swim platform where the tender was tied. Willow used the opportunity to control assigning the tanks, reserving the marked one for Zach. Once the student had received hers, she lingered and tried to engage Zach in conversation, stepping into his personal space and talking softly so that he would have to lean in.

Zach, however, was wise to the machinations of young women and stepped away, turning to the tall blonde deckhand he had met yesterday and receiving his tank from her.

Pretending that he hadn't realized the student, Mindy he thought her name was, had been trying to speak to him, he addressed the crewmember, "So you will be driving the dive boat for us today, Willow?"

Dispensing the last tank and picking up a spare in each hand, she held them by the nozzle and started moving aft. "Sure thing, Professor. Let's make it a great trip," she said, trying to keep things professional.

She went first onto the launch and turned the engine over. Once it was humming smoothly, Willow gestured for everyone to come aboard. She took the gear from each person as they stepped down into the smaller boat. Willow was careful to keep one eye on Zach's gear throughout the loading process. The barely clad Mindy made a show of needing help and trying to hang onto Zach. He was gracious and helped her out but quickly distanced himself once they were in the boat, choosing instead to stand alongside Willow as she took one last look around and asked, "Everybody clear?"

Hearing no objections, she nodded to the crew member on the deck who threw her mooring line at her in a neat coil. Then, she engaged the motor and began carefully backing away from the larger vessel. Turning to Zach, she asked, "Where to, Professor?"

Zach had a GPS around his neck and powered it up as he replied, "Head off to the east and I'll guide you."

CHAPTER SIX

The fact that this was likely the time where the professor was to die had Willow on edge. A short time later, Zach held up a hand, indicating that the launch had reached their destination. Because the ocean was so deep at this point, the chain necessary to reach the bottom with an anchor would be more than the small boat could carry. So, Willow disengaged the engine. She would periodically make the adjustments necessary to keep the craft at the set coordinates. To the student sitting next to the short flagpole at the back of the boat she asked, "Would you run up the dive flag, please?" This would alert other boats motoring through the area, if there were any, that the launch had divers in the water.

Because there were beginner divers in the group, they would all be using a full-face dive mask with a radio built in. That would allow them to keep in contact with each other and with Willow at the surface. After conducting a radio check with her and each member of the team, Zach made sure that all the students had their dive bags with their sample collection equipment ready. He then instructed them to don their gear. The less experienced divers would be staying closer to the boat where the current was less of a challenge. Once they had flipped off the gunwale and were in the water, Zach and the other team made their preparations.

Willow was nervous. She was glad that she would be able to communicate with each diver and hear their communications with each other. Still, she would be at a disadvantage if an act of sabotage occurred underwater. She had brought along the extra tanks and gear with the excuse of replacing something faulty. However, she would also be able to quickly slip into the equipment and get to Zach's rescue if need be. However, if something happened suddenly, she wouldn't have time to come to his aid. If he wasn't able to shout an alarm, she would never know he needed help. Thankfully, none of the team members were carrying spear guns.

The second team, including Zach, were now in the water and then everyone sank below the surface and Willow was alone. The lapping of the waves and the rumble of the inboard the only sounds keeping her company. A short time later, chatter on the radio started as the various team members reported their status. With bated breath, Willow willed Zach to respond and a wave of relief washed over her when she heard the deep timber of his voice. With a big sigh, she realized she would be a nervous wreck before the dive was over.

The student group had collected their water samples and reported that they were headed back to the launch. Zach's team was working into the stronger current and reporting that everything was going according to schedule. None of the divers had reached the surface yet when movement in the waves caught Willow's eye. A grey fin was slicing through the water. It didn't have the bobbing movement of dolphins. Suddenly, Willow's heart was in her throat as she keyed the radio, "We've got a shark at the surface."

Scanning around, she saw another fin, and then a third. "Make that sharks. They seem to be circling around the boat," she reported.

Zach's voice broke in on the radio with authority. "Everyone, stay calm. Does anyone have eyes on any sharks near them?"

A chorus of 'no's' came over the radio.

Zach continued, his voice full of calm authority, "There is no need for panic. I want divers to ascend one person at a time. Stay down if you can unless you start to see sharks around you. They are likely attracted to the boat thinking we are fishing. When each diver swims up, try to keep the splashing and flailing to a minimum. That will only excite the sharks more."

The usual practice for divers was to surface and then swim the remaining distance to the dive boat. The boat was too difficult to visualize from underwater unless one was directly underneath it. It was much easier to visually find the craft once the diver was above water. However, the sharks swimming around the boat would make it very dangerous for exposed divers making their way on the surface. Moving the boat wasn't likely to improve the situation as the sharks would just follow along.

With a sudden idea, Willow broke onto the radio, "Professor, I'll slowly let the anchor down so that each diver can use it to ascend right at the boat and keep the water turbulence to a minimum." Continuing to think as she spoke, she added, "I'll secure a dive flashlight to the chain so you will be able to find it easier at depth."

Zach's reply was immediate. "That's a great idea, Willow! Not being horizontal at the surface will make everyone look less like prey to the sharks. Let us know when you have the anchor down. I want every diver to find a partner and buddy up."

Willow grabbed duct tape from the launch's tool kit and a waterproof flashlight. Then, she used the anchor's motor to slowly lower the weight until all the chain was in the water.

"Okay, anchor's out," she announced over the radio. "Can anyone see it?"

Several of the divers reported visuals and headed towards it. The student group was closest and soon announced their arrival.

Still making his way in the gloom, Zach instructed the biggest male student to go first, "Mason, you lead the way. We'll need a big strong guy to help haul everybody in." Because the swim ladder was at the back of the boat and the anchor was at the bow, which was higher off the waterline, each person at the surface would struggle to get out. Agitating the water would draw the attention of the sharks. Having someone strong in the bow to help lift the drivers up quickly would be important. Willow would have to do the job all alone with Mason and he was a big guy. The first person would be the greatest test.

Mason didn't hesitate or argue. He just replied, "Yes, sir."

Zach had joined up with the more expert divers in his team and soon saw a glimmer in the murky shadows in front of him. Then, the other students' forms took shape. With an internal sigh of relief, he realized everyone was accounted for. Now, if they could just get everyone back on the boat without incident.

Most sharks were naturally curious but a lot of thrashing or blood in the water would quickly have them in a frenzy. Mentally, Zach had resolved that he would be the last person out of the water. He tried to slow his breathing to conserve his air. The students were likely hyperventilating and would soon have empty tanks. "Slow breaths everyone. I want a status report from each diver regarding how much air each of you have left."

The other divers chimed in and Zach arranged their ascent in order of least remaining air. They had watched Mason climb the chain to the surface. He didn't linger long before his flippers disappeared.

Zach asked, "Ready for another one?"

Willow responded right away, "Sure thing."

The next student began their climb and was soon hoisted aboard the launch. Zach could see the long bodies of the sharks suspended near the surface as they continued to slowly circle the boat and a chill ran down his spine. He was trying to project confidence for his students, but any time sharks were involved, his nerves were on edge.

Several more students had made the trip successfully and the sharks had not increased their lazy circling. Then it was Mindy's turn. She quickly rose to the surface but, once there, began thrashing around as she seemed to have trouble getting into the boat. The attention of the sharks was drawn to the area and the shadowy shapes quickly knifed their way toward the water around the anchor.

Willow had turned the job of helping people back into the boat over to a couple of the students and was using her weight to counterbalance their efforts. Then, as more people were back in the vessel, she rummaged around in the storage under the bench seats. Finding what she wanted, she headed back to the bow of the boat.

Just as she arrived, Mindy was being hauled on board. She was screaming and flailing and kicked her flippers vigorously as she tried to climb in.

Anger washed over Willow at the foolish young woman

and she snapped, "Settle down. You're safe now but you've made a fine mess for everyone else still down there."

Removing her fins, Mindy shrugged out of her tanks and rushed to the gunwale, causing the boat to rock a bit. Willow adjusted her stance and directed in a tone that brooked no argument, "Get to the back of the boat and stay there."

Mindy hesitated, glanced at the water around the anchor and then complied.

Willow watched her go and turned back to Mason and the other young man. "I found a shock stick. It may be enough to deter any of the sharks that come at divers when they're at the surface."

Keying the radio, she updated the remaining divers, "Let's give the sharks a few minutes to see if they calm down. I found a shock stick and I'll try to drive off any of them that get too bold."

Zach did the calculations in his head. It was going to be close whether or not he was going to have enough air when it was his turn. Waiting for the sharks to settle back down may not be an option for him. The knot of fear grew in his stomach. "Roger that," was his short reply.

Trying to conserve his air further, he signaled the next divers to begin their ascent. Trying to speed things along, before the next diver had reached to top, he instructed another to start climbing. Zach could see that the long dark silhouettes were circling more quickly but, as yet, had made no move on the divers.

Finally, Zach was the only one remaining at the anchor, watching the last person make their way to the surface. The edges of his vision were starting to grow darker in the dim water as he looked up toward the bottom of the boat.

Trying to keep his breathing slow, he pulled himself up the anchor chain hand over hand. His muscles were burning with the effort and he concentrated his vision on the links in front of his mask. Looking around for the sharks would have been a waste of precious energy.

He willed himself to keep the motion going, hand over hand over hand. It felt as though he was never going to reach the surface. Zach's lungs were on fire and he was gasping for breath in his face mask. Through his dimming vision, he thought the hull of the boat was finally right above him. With one last herculean lunge upward, his head broke the surface. Ripping the mask off, Zach gulped in huge breaths and felt the burning in his lungs start to abate. Strength started to flow back into his lax muscles.

Zach heard yelling above him, and arms were reaching down to grab the straps of his tank, pulling him upwards. The was a sound near his shoulder that he realized was the shock stick being deployed. As Zach was lifted upward, he felt a shove at his hip. As it registered, he realized that it was likely the tail of a shark as it was turned away by the electricity since there wasn't an accompanying burning pain of a bite.

Zach was now lying on his stomach, suspended over the gunwale, as his rescuers kept pulling his tall frame aboard. There suddenly was a tugging on his foot and he felt himself being drawn backward. He sensed movement and saw Willow leaning over his legs and heard the shock stick again. Then, the force on his foot was gone and he slid to the wet deck of the bow, gasping for breath. Amazingly, all the team had made it back aboard, apparently without injury.

As Zach looked up, he saw Willow wielding the shark prod and realized that without her quick thinking, this would have likely had a very different outcome. Weakly, between gasps for air, he murmured, "Thank you."

He thought he saw real concern and fear in her eyes for a second before she asked, "Are you okay, Professor?"

He just nodded, weak from lack of oxygen and the quickly abating adrenaline.

Willow wanted to check him out more thoroughly but didn't want her concern to seem obvious, so she turned back toward the wheel and said, "Then I'm going to get us back to the *Learn of the Sea*."

Zach looked down at his swim fin and saw that a large portion of the plastic was missing, forming a gaping hole. Sliding it off, he saw no bite marks on his skin. Miraculously, the razor-like teeth had just missed his foot.

It seemed like only minutes later and the dive tender was pulling up to the aft deck of the bigger ship. The launch was abuzz with excited voices as the students recounted their perspectives of their adventure with the sharks. Willow threw a line to another member of the deck crew who quickly tied it off to a cleat. As everyone was climbing off the boat, Zach hung back so that he would be the last one off.

Touching Willow on the elbow, he said, "I really can't thank you enough for your quick thinking. That situation could easily have ended horribly. The team and I owe you our lives. Would you mind joining me for dinner in my cabin tonight?"

Willow was surprised and a tingle of pleasure radiated up her arm from where his light touch cupped her elbow and landed in a flutter in her core. Pleased, before she could think about the merits of getting close to her charge, she agreed, "I just did what anyone else would have. But, yes, I'd like to join you."

She watched Zach climb out of the boat and walk away before she turned to the deck crew and began to unload the used dive gear. Willow wanted time to process the morning's events but there was more work to be done. And, now, having thwarted what had been a previously sccessful attack on the professor, she would be blind to the nature of the next one.

CHAPTER SEVEN

2018, Atlantic Ocean off the coast of the United States

In the evening, Willow's duties on deck were finally finished. She had been dismissed for the night, so she headed to Zach's cabin. She felt an unexpected nervous flutter in her stomach as she knocked on the door.

Zach opened it promptly and Willow said, "Hi there. I wasn't sure if you were serious about that dinner offer. You really don't have to, you know."

Zach's reply was quick and accompanied by a wide smile, "Of course I meant the invitation! Thank you for coming," he said as he opened the door wide and gestured with his arm for her to enter.

"I asked the cook to make some cold things for us since I didn't know when you would be coming. I hope that is alright with you?" he continued.

Walking in, Willow smiled and nodded reassuringly,

"Sounds perfect," she responded.

After they were seated, Zach uncovered a large bowl of salad and a plate of sandwiches. As he motioned for her to help herself to the food, he spoke up again, "While I appreciate that you don't want to take credit for your quick thinking today, I really can't thank you enough for what you did. As a professor, I don't want to have to medivac students with shark bites to the mainland and then have to explain everything to the school. More importantly, I would hate to have to tell their parents. Personally, I have to admit that I was dangerously close to being out of air and only your use of the shock stick kept me from being bitten. As it was, only my fin was a casualty. I think that you deserve way more than a simple 'thank you'."

Uncomfortable with his praise, Willow looked down at her plate and mumbled, "You're welcome, Zach. I'd like to think that any of the crew would have done the same."

Seeing her discomfort, Zach searched for another topic, "How's the food?'

Taking a couple of bites before she answered gave her time to settle her unexpected nerves. "Good," she eventually replied. Because she was genuinely interested, she asked, "Would you mind telling me more about your work with the algae?"

Zach lit up and launched into details about his plan. He described how he had worked with a geneticist to modify his strain of algae. He shared his vision for having a supertanker specially outfitted with the glass tubes parked next to the massive floating islands of garbage that had formed in the oceans. He wanted to clean the waters at the site while other vessels worked on removing the larger pieces of debris.

The algae reprocessed the microplastics back into a crude byproduct which was siphoned off. It could be collected in the hold of the supertanker and transported back to the mainland where it could be refined. Willow was impressed with Zach's enthusiasm and knowledge on the topic. It was such a shame that the petrochemical companies were more interested in suppressing his discovery rather than utilizing it. Having cleaner water and a passively produced byproduct would be cheaper than pumping oil out of the ground.

She spoke up with the observation, "It seems as though your process would be cheaper than all the fracking and exploration to keep pumping oil out of the ground. You should have companies beating down your door to get their hands on your algae."

Zach shook his head ruefully. "I would have thought so too. But, as it turns out, even though I offered to donate specimens of the algae so that companies could grow their own, no one is taking me up on it. Some companies want to buy the exclusive rights to my process but then it couldn't be mass produced."

Willow was impressed that Zach wasn't looking to make money from his discovery. Wondering if there was a longer endgame in his plan, she pressed him, "But if you give it away, what do you get out of your work? Notoriety?"

Zach looked a little sheepish, "I guess that might happen but, really, I just want cleaner oceans. The microplastics are getting into the fish people eat. People will start to have problems with microplastics in their bodies too, the longer this continues. If I can do something to makes a difference, that is the only reward I need."

Willow couldn't help being impressed but she also realized that this mindset was what had led to the professor's death in the previous timeline. Because he genuinely cared, he couldn't be bought off. Her anger at the petrochemical companies seethed and she tried to hide it as she said, "I hope that you can find someone to work with because it really sounds like you could make a difference."

The short-sightedness and greed of the corporate CEOs would negatively impact the human race for generations and the average person was helpless to impact it. She appreciated that Zach was pushing ahead anyway and trying to use his knowledge to make the world a better place. The people in her time were only now beginning to be able to eat fish and other ocean creatures. However, the biodiversity of the eco-system had been decimated by the microplastics so there were still places that were devoid of sea life.

Zach replied, "I hope so, too."

Deciding that she would offer a bit of a warning, Willow asked, "Are you at all worried that one of those companies might want to keep you from sharing your discovery?"

Zach met her eyes, stunned by the idea. After a moment, he shook his head and countered with a question of his own, "Why would they want to do that? I'm helping to clean up their mess and any company that uses my process would have a tanker full of crude that didn't cost them anything if they used solar-powered water pumps on the tanker. Seems like that would make it profitable for any company that wanted to try it."

Willow nodded, backing off and letting him digest the thought. "I hear you, but it seems sometimes that these companies can't see the bigger picture. They just want to do business the way they have always done it and they know the profit is a sure thing."

Zach sighed and his shoulders sagged a bit as he thought about the lack of interest in his concept, "That's for sure," he agreed.

The rest of their evening passed too quickly and, since

Willow had to be up early for her duties on deck, she needed to head back to her bunk. She was surprised that she was reluctant to wrap up her time with Zach. As she rose to leave, he gently reached out a hand to rest on her forearm. At the innocent contact, a frisson of awareness coursed through her, rooting her feet to the floor.

Zach was aware that he didn't want their time together to end and it was a unique feeling for him. Clearing his throat, he murmured, "Um, this is really unlike me, especially during the middle of a research trip. I don't normally get too friendly with the crew or my students. But, Willow, I really enjoyed talking with you tonight and I wondered if you would mind joining me for dinner again tomorrow?"

Without pausing to consider the wisdom, Willow agreed, "I'd like that very much."

Before she did anything impulsive like kiss those mobile lips of his that had beckoned her all evening across their makeshift dinner table, she crossed quickly to the door and made her exit. As she was closing the door, she couldn't help adding, "I'll be looking forward to it."

Then, with the door separating them, she let out a deep breath. She needed to be careful. For the mission, she needed to be close to Zach so fostering an association between them was good for the job. However, spending a lot of time with the professor was going to make it difficult for her to keep her growing attraction to the man under control.

The following day, despite looking for her frequently,

Zach didn't see much of Willow. He had several of his students running multiple tests on the samples they had collected. Others on the team were tasked with running diagnostics on the algae replication rates and adjusting flow rates in an effort to determine optimum function of the experiment.

Toward the end of the afternoon, as Zach had his mind on another evening with Willow, the compiled test results were printed and handed to him for review. Looking them over, the mass spectrometer results caught his attention and he was no longer thinking about dinner. He checked the results again and asked to see the samples. After careful inspection, he thanked the students and dismissed everyone for the night.

A short while later, when Willow knocked on his cabin door, Zach absentmindedly bade her to enter. She found him deeply occupied with a series of graphs spread out on his bunk.

"If you would rather, I can eat in the crew mess," she offered. "It looks like you have a lot of material in front of you."

Zach didn't look up from the sheaf of papers in his hand and waved absently toward the table, "No, no. Help yourself."

He still couldn't believe what he was seeing and, with sudden inspiration said, "Willow, you are an experienced diver. I'd like to get your opinion on something that I can't make sense of on one of the samples collected yesterday."

Flattered that he would want to share his research with her she replied, "Sure. What would you like me to look at?"

Zach just handed her the stack of papers and asked, "What do you see?"

Willow realized she was looking at a spectral analysis graph and there were the usual mineral spikes. However, there were several chemical spikes on the other side of the graph. Her attention was now focused on the sheet too. The chemicals present were the common ingredients for two substances. One was shark repellant and the other was blood scent formulated to attract them.

Puzzled, she asked, "These were both in the same sample?"

Zach nodded and replied, "Yeah, I can't understand how the samples got contaminated. I gave all my divers specific instructions to shower before the diver and not wear any chemicals."

At his words, the pieces fell into place for Willow and she knew, without a doubt, that the sharks congregating around their boat the day before had been lured there. It had been a bold move to try to make it look like an accidental shark attack. Her mind spun and she thought further. The saboteur must have been one of the divers. When they saw that their plan to empty Zach's tank hadn't worked, they had moved to another tactic. Getting into the water with frenzied sharks would be dangerous so the guilty party had slathered themselves with repellent. They obviously hadn't thought about the chemicals being collected along with their water samples, though.

That led to an idea and Willow asked, "Who collected the samples?" hoping that it would point a finger at the assassin.

If she identified the person, she would be successful in her assignment. When the AIs determined that her mission was successful and the professor was safe, her communicator would alert her. Then, she would have to find a reason to leave the ship in the middle of the voyage. A pang of disappointment washed over her at that thought. With a mental shrug, she convinced herself that it was just wanting to see if the algae experiments would be successful.

Zach shook his head and replied, "That is what is really confusing me. They are the samples that I collected. I know that I didn't have either of those substances on me and part of the prep the students did was to wipe all of the dive equipment down before we conducted the dive."

Willow's excitement fell flat. So much for the hope that it would lead back to their culprit. After a moment's consideration, she asked. "Since it is safe to say it wasn't you, could we go back to the sample tubes and inspect the labels? Maybe they were switched by whoever did it to try to hide their tracks."

Zach brightened at the idea, "Sure!" He took her arm by the elbow and headed for the door, their meal forgotten on his desk. Willow was as eager to find the answer and was happy to tag along.

When they arrived at the lab, it was empty with all the metal countertops wiped clean. Crossing to a refrigerator, Zach opened it and pulled out a rack with sample tubes standing neatly side by side. Each had a number on the side and he quickly found the vials they needed. Pulling one from the rack, he held it up to the light. Very clearly, they could see that the number label had been peeled off and replaced.

"Maybe whoever did it switched them with their own to try to cover their tracks," she suggested.

"Good idea," Zach said as he replaced the glass tube and pulled out the first one in the rack. Holding it up to the light, his face fell. The label was also tampered with. Sliding it back in place, he randomly selected another, looked and repeated the process several more times in silence as his movements became more frantic.

As he realized that all the samples had been renumbered, a wave of disappointment washed over him. Not only was the search a dead end, it also revealed that all the information he and the team had risked their life for was now useless. Frustration rose up and he wanted to pitch the whole rack in the trash, but he refrained.

Willow could see that the samples had all been re-labeled and that any hope of finding the person responsible for bringing the sharks around the boat was quickly fading. Doggedly, she asked, "Who were the students conducting the tests today? Maybe one of them switched everything around."

Zach shook his head, "I assigned two students to each lab task to keep anyone from cutting corners on the analyses. It would be hard to explain something like that to the other person. All the students were in here at various times to complete their assignments. It could be any one of them. What I don't understand is, why? Why would anyone sabotage the experiments?"

Trying to shrink the pool of potential suspects, Willow asked, "Is the lab locked at night?"

Zach shook his head again and she realized that they knew little more now than when they had started. Anyone, including members of the crew or the divers on Zach's team, could have snuck into the room during the night. The presence of the chemicals pointed to one of the divers, either student or the experienced professionals that had been diving with Zach in the stronger current. However, there was a real possibility that the person wasn't working alone, and their partner might have been the one to switch the labels in the lab.

With a sigh of frustration, Willow suggested, "Why don't we go back to your room and eat while we talk this out."

On the way back to the cabin, Willow had a lot to ponder. Once they were seated, they began eating their salad and sandwiches, absorbed in their own thoughts.

Willow reached a decision and broke the silence. Starting with a partial truth, she asked, "Zach, have you considered that maybe someone is deliberately trying to sabotage your algae experiment and maybe even harm you?"

Zach's eyes flew from his plate of food to meet her steady gaze. "Why on Earth would anyone want to do that?"

"Well, maybe one of the companies you offered the process to feels threatened somehow and wants to sweep it under the rug, so to speak."

Seeing his incredulous expression, she forged on, "I mean, if you had been killed yesterday by one of the sharks, would your algae and the scrubbing process die with you?"

"Yes, I suppose so." Zach argued, "But why would anyone want to keep us from cleaning up the oceans?"

"Companies that are making a lot of money pumping crude oil might feel threatened that your process makes it as a byproduct at no cost. Perhaps that would be enough incentive, particularly since you are offering it for free. They wouldn't be able to control the market," she speculated.

Zach felt a shiver of fear run down his spine. Willow actually presented a convincing argument and he realized in that moment that the presence of the sharks had been directed at him. It would have looked like an accident, but it could also have taken out any number of his students as well.

He looked earnestly into her eyes and said, "Thank you so much for your quick thinking. I owe you not just my life. If one of the students had been harmed, it would have been a major blow to my professional reputation which also could have tainted the algae project."

Since he was grasping the situation, Willow decided to press a little more, "Maybe you should cancel the class and send all the students back to shore with the next supply delivery."

Zach quickly responded with a vigorous shake of his

head, "I can't do that. I have to meet my obligation to the university. However, I won't risk having any of them in the water again, that's for sure! I'll keep the expeditions smaller, just the ship's divers and myself. And I can have the students collect samples from the launch."

Seeing Zach's determined expression, she doubted she would be able to change his mind, but Willow decided to share the last bit of information she had. "I hope it's just coincidence, but when I was inspecting your dive equipment yesterday morning, I found your tank almost empty. I refilled it and kept an eye on it, in case there was a malfunctioning valve. That's why I brought along a couple spare tanks. In light of our suspicions, you probably should consider that it had been deliberately drained. From now on, you should service your own gear and keep it here in your cabin. I presume that you can lock this door and that no one else has the key?"

Zach shook his head, "No there's a master key that Captain Harvey keeps on the bridge and I have no idea who else would have access to it. But I do have a secure locker I had the algae shipped here in. I'll have it brought in here and keep my gear in it. That's a really good idea. Thank you, Willow." His mind was reeling from the news that his gear had been tampered with. He realized that he had another reason to thank her for saving his life.

By this time, they had finished their meal and it was getting late. Willow was on early duty again the next day. She was reluctant to leave but pushed away from the table and stood, "Zach, if you are determined to keep working, you really need to be careful and not take unnecessary risks," she said as she walked to the door.

Zach followed, reluctant for her to leave. His mind was spinning with so many revelations and he doubted he would get much sleep that night. It seemed surreal that someone was actually trying to kill him. He knew that he should feel more afraid than he did. Perhaps, later when it really sank in, he would. However, he felt that there was one person he could trust in all this and that was Willow. She was levelheaded and he was having a hard time fighting his attraction to her.

Lightly cupping her elbow, he turned her toward him and murmured, "I really appreciate your help. I know that I've already said it, but I would have died if you hadn't been thinking quickly. I don't normally get involved with anyone while I'm working, but I can't seem to resist you. I'd really like to kiss you right now."

Willow felt Zach's arms gently slide around her as she lifted her lips and Zach lowered his mouth. Their lips met with a soft touch and Willow felt like a bolt of electricity had coursed through her. Zach had wanted to keep things low-key between them but when his lips came in contact with her mouth, he felt like he had been shoved off-balance. Instinctively, he deepened the kiss, pressing firmly on her mobile mouth, staking his claim.

Willow felt like every sense in her body was focused on Zach. His lips on hers were hot and hungry. She felt her pulse begin racing and tried to catch her breath, but she only inhaled his spicy scent which sent every rational thought about why this was a bad idea, flying out of her head. Surrendering to the delightful way he was making her feel, Willow drew her arms around Zach and savored the way his tongue dipped inside to duel with hers.

After several delicious minutes, Willow reminded herself that she had a job to do to keep this man safe. She was reluctant as she gently eased away and said, "I admit, I feel attracted to you too, Zach. But I have to work in the morning."

As she slipped out the door, she couldn't resist whispering, "I wouldn't mind picking up where we left off sometime soon."

A few minutes later, she was laying in her bunk, reliving the pressure of his lips and the feel of his arms around her. The attraction she was feeling for Zach was an unexpected complication to her mission. It would be foolish for her to give in to her feelings. She harshly reminded herself that there could be no future for them.

CHAPTER EIGHT

The next day, Willow was up at dawn, working on her assigned tasks about the ship. She helped the cook prepare breakfast for the crew and determined that she would encourage Zach to eat with everyone else going forward because it would be too easy for someone to slip poison into the meals being sent to his cabin. It would also be a good way for her keep her distance from the professor and keep her mind on her mission. Despite her best efforts, Willow found her mind wandering to the feel of his lips on hers when she should have been thinking about what form the next attack might take.

The day passed uneventfully as Zach oversaw the students collecting new samples and analyzing them. He seemed to be taking the threat seriously as he stayed on the ship while the team went out in the launch. She was able to share her recommendation about eating with the crew but otherwise, her duties kept her away from him most of the day.

After dinner, Willow was off duty and retreated to a quiet spot on the foredeck and watched the sun set. Her thoughts were a jumbled mess as she reminded herself that she couldn't have any future with a man from what was history to her.

The ship wasn't big enough to hide anywhere for long. As if thinking about him conjured his presence, Zach found her just after the sun had gone down and the shadows were gathering on deck.

Zach figured Willow was off duty and wondered if she was avoiding him because she was uncomfortable facing him. She had only had a few words for him all day. When he found her near the bow, he decided to face the possibility head on. "Do you mind if I join you? I hope that you aren't hiding from me after our kiss," he said to open the conversation.

Willow shook her head and smiled. Even though that had been the case, she quickly forgot her resolve as soon as they were alone together. "No. Have a seat," she beckoned to a spot near her. She was using the locker where one of the life rafts were stored as her bench.

Zach took a seat and said, "I've had some time to think today. I know that there is plenty of evidence to the contrary, but I really still can't understand why anyone would want to keep my discovery from the world. It wouldn't do anything but help make the Earth a better, safer place to pass on to the next generation."

Willow had been thinking about his algae also. "I know that you have focused on cleaning up the oceans with your process. But, would there also be the potential application on land? Could you build a permanent facility that could turn plastics in landfills into crude?"

Zach thought for a moment and said, "I don't' see why not. The plastics would have to be finely ground before the algae could process them, but I guess that could be done."

After another moment's consideration, he grew enthusiastic. Reaching for her arm, Zach hypothesized, "Imagine being able to clean up all the massive landfills around the world!"

Willow felt the heat of his hand and was pleased that he was considering her idea. In the shadows, she thought she saw a movement and a tiny glint of light. Moving reflexively, she drew Zach down onto the deck in a sudden forceful move. He landed with a grunt alongside her and there was a solid 'thunk' as something forcefully hit the wood where they had been sitting only a moment ago. Willow quickly spun back toward the spot where she had seen the movement. She saw that a fishing spear was now firmly embedded in the wood of the locker.

Zach sat up and saw the spear. Aware that he had been seated in that spot moments before, a wave of fear washed over him.

Willow broke the silence. "Well, it seems that whoever is behind these attacks is growing more desperate. They don't seem worried about making it look like you had an accident anymore."

Speechless, Zach shook his head, but Willow didn't see the movement as she kept her eyes trained on the shadows behind them.

"We need to get out of the open," she said, feeling exposed where they were.

She grabbed Zach by the arm and said, "Stay close to me," as she helped him up. Then Willow hurried him back to his cabin where she locked the door behind them. She was already kicking herself for the way that she had allowed her distraction to jeopardize her mission.

Zach began pacing the room. "I think we should tell Captain Harvey about our suspicions."

Willow objected, sharing a little more of what she knew, "Probably, but are you sure that we can trust him? If your process is a threat to the current petrochemical companies' way of doing business, they could be willing to spend a lot of money to silence you. They could have gotten to anyone."

Zach continued pacing, "I understand what you are saying, but even though someone is obviously trying to kill me, I just can't believe this is happening! Maybe there is some other explanation."

Because the corporate connection wasn't a totally proven theory in the historical record, even though the evidence was strong, she asked, "Do you have a jilted lover or a jealous husband of a lover that would want you dead?"

Zach looked at her, surprised, before answering honestly, "No, certainly none that I know of. I don't get tangled up with married women and I thought that my last several relationships ended agreeably."

Willow pressed him, "Maybe a former student that is stalking you? Have any of the people in this class taken other classes from you?"

Zach knew that students sometimes became infatuated with their professors. He answered promptly though, "No, all the students on board are new to me."

Willow tried to use logic to make her point, "Then, unless you can think of some other reason a person on this boat is trying to kill you, I think that we can be comfortable assuming that all of this is an attempt to silence your algae discovery." She decided to introduce an idea that would make her protection job easier, "Maybe you should consider leaving the boat."

Zach shook his head vehemently at the notion, "No way! I'm not going to run from this. Besides, I have students that are expecting a class. The University won't like it if I cut my class short. We've just barely gotten started. And, if I don't finish my experiments, I won't have the proof that my algae can function as I think they will."

The last point made Willow pause, "Do you think that the person's next attempt may be to sabotage the algae tubes?"

Zach shuddered at the thought. "I have no idea, but it is probably something to consider."

"Well, I think that is a good reason to talk to the Captain as you had suggested. Maybe you should also consider keeping a sample safely here in your cabin too."

Zach nodded and picked up the phone in his room. It was a direct line to the bridge, and he asked Captain Harvey to come to his cabin.

When the man arrived, they presented their evidence as to the problems that had been going on and their concerns about the algae experiment. While the Captain was disbelieving at first, when he heard about the spear incident, he left them to go see for himself.

A few minutes later, Captain Harvey returned. He said that the spear was no longer where they had indicated, but he did see the mark in the wood of the storage locker. He said that the evidence had changed his mind. Willow decided to test his reaction by bringing up the possibility of a large petroleum company trying to suppress Zach's process for financial gain, and he nodded, considering. The captain didn't seem at all nervous during their conversation. She suggested that a guard be posted and, as the Captain left to make the arrangements, she felt reasonably sure that he wasn't involved.

Willow decided to check her communicator to see if the recent developments had changed the outcome in the future and if Zach was now safe, but her screen still flashed red and displayed a large 0% as an indication of percentage of success of her mission. With a small sigh of disappointment, she turned back to Zach. He was still pacing around the small room.

Willow tried again to see if she could get him to change his mind about leaving the ship, "Is there another professor or a teacher's assistant who could be flown out to take over, even just for a few days? It might be a way to flush out your assassin. Once you have left the ship, they would also want to get off to follow you, thinking that you weren't coming back. Then, when they are caught, you could come back and resume your work."

Zach paused to consider her idea. He realized it had merit and conceded, "I'll send an email to a couple people to see if I can work something out. But just for a few days."

Not wanting to lose the momentum, she urged, "Why don't you send those messages right now."

Zach sat down at his desk and woke up his laptop. There was limited access to the ship's Wi-Fi, but, as senior faculty, he could send and receive messages. In moments, his fingers were tapping across the keyboard.

Willow distracted herself by inspecting the small collection of books that he had stacked atop the dresser in the corner. It was surprising to find several works of science fiction among the textbooks. Picking one up, she read the blurb on the back cover and was intrigued. Making a note, she resolved to try to find it when she got back to her time since it looked like an interesting story.

She caught a whiff of smoke and turned toward the door, only to see puffs billowing from underneath it. "Fire!" she yelled at Zach who stopped typing and sprang to his feet. She rushed to the door and felt it with the back of her hand. It was hot to the touch, so they were blocked from their only way of escape. "Call the bridge!" she ordered as she rushed to the tiny adjoining bathroom. There she grabbed a stack of towels and threw them on the shower floor before opening the taps.

As she worked, she heard Zach shout from the other room, "The line is dead. I can't reach anyone."

Willow's hand searched for the radio on her belt but realized that, since she was off duty, she had put it on a charging base for the night. Scooping up the sodden pile of towels, she rushed back to the door and threw them at the base. That, at least temporarily, stopped the flow of choking smoke into the room. Starting a fire on a ship so far from land was a desperate or stupid move. Willow was hopeful that there wouldn't be much fuel for the fire since so much of the vessel was metal.

She crossed to one of the portholes in the opposite wall and threw it open and began yelling, "FIRE! FIRE on the ship! FIRE!"

Zach followed her move and added his voice to the alarm.

Relief washed over Willow as, moments later, the fire alarm began blaring throughout the vessel and she could hear feet pounding down the corridor outside the room.

Only a short time later, the door was swinging open and one of the crew stuck his head inside to ask, "Everyone okay in here?"

Zach bolted out the door and Willow paused to answer, "Yes, all good. Thanks for getting the fire out so quickly," as she rushed after him.

She figured that Zach was headed to check on his experiment. The fire would have provided an excellent diversion to ruin the equipment, but she worried that someone might be standing by with another spear gun and he could be rushing headlong into a trap.

When Zach arrived at the middeck, his eyes went immediately to the tall glass tubes. Sure enough, the water level was rapidly falling in all of them as the valves had been opened wide. The guards that had just been posted had left to fight the fire and someone had used the opportunity to drain the tubes containing Zach's precious algae into the ocean.

Heedless of the danger, he rushed over to the valves and began furiously spinning them closed again. Willow arrived on his heels and watched the shadows around the deck for any sign of another attempt on Zach's life.

Relief flooded through Zach as the last valve closed. He had lost some of the algae but there was still plenty remaining in the tubes. As he reached for a nearby bucket, he thought about having to report the spill to the school and international scientific societies. It had not been his intention to release the algae without approval from the oceanological community. There could be unintended effects on the ecosystem, and he worried as he syphoned off the small sample he would keep in his cabin.

When he was finished, Zach turned back to Willow who grabbed him by the arm and hurried him to the kitchen.

"I presume you will need a jar or some container to put your sample in?" she asked once they were there.

Zach looked through several cupboards until he found what he wanted. As he worked, he listened to Willow on the ship's phone, talking to the Captain. Since his cabin door had been ruined by the fire set right outside it, she was making arrangements for a new cabin for him.

Once the algae sample had been secured, Willow hustled Zach back to his room and instructed him to pack all his gear. Since there was just his computer, a few clothes and his books, he was quickly finished.

The Captain came through the charred doorway and apologized for the guards' deserting their post to fight the fire and he showed them to another cabin just down the corridor that had been quickly vacated by the first mate.

"I'm sorry to be kicking someone out of their bunk," Zach said as he walked into the room carrying his gear.

"Nonsense." Captain Harvey replied. "You obviously need to be in a secure location until we can find out who is behind all this. I'm going to be posting a guard outside your door and back on your experiment. This time, they will be instructed not to leave their post for any reason." With that, he left the room and closed the door behind him.

Alone again for the first time since all the excitement had begun, Zach turned to Willow and said, "It looks like I'm thanking you yet again for saving my life and my experiment. Thank you hardly seems adequate anymore. You really have a way with thinking on your feet."

Willow deflected his praise, "I'm sure anyone would have done the same things."

Zach shook his head, "I don't think so. I probably would have stood looking at that smoke for another minute before I would have thought to wet down the towels."

"Well, I'm just glad that someone heard us yelling and put out the fire. It could have spread and put everyone on the ship in danger."

Wanting to change the subject, she said, "Zach, I really feel like you should have an extra set of eyes and ears around you right now. Your discovery is important, and it needs to be given to the world to make the oceans healthier. How would you feel about my staying here with you tonight?"

From a personal perspective, she wasn't sure that she was making the smartest suggestion. She would figure out a way to keep her focus on her mission and not the man standing in front of her. Before he could get the wrong impression, she added, "I can sleep in the chair," as she waved at the desk chair nearby.

Zach looked skeptically at that option and shook his head, "While I appreciate the offer, I can sleep on the floor and you can take the bed."

Feeling guilty, Willow hesitated. The idea of being close to Zach was probably a mistake and she was probably digging herself into deeper trouble as she said, "Or, we could be two adults and just share the bed."

Zach ground his teeth and mentally resolved to keep his hands off. If she could do it, so could he. "Okay. Problem solved," he pronounced.

Since it was getting late and she would have to turn in soon, she realized she would need to go back to her bunk for some PJs. "Um. Problem number two, I need to go to my cabin for a change of clothes."

"Or, if you want, you could just borrow one of my t-shirts to sleep in," Zach offered.

While she could make the errand quick, she hated to be away, even briefly, given the way that Zach seemed to be attracting trouble. After a brief consideration, she agreed to his offer.

Zach unpacked his duffle, putting things away in the dresser as he went. When he came to a t-shirt that he thought might fit her, he handed it to Willow.

She stepped into the bathroom and quickly changed, leaving her underpants on since she knew the t-shirt would ride up in her sleep. She used some mouthwash and wished she had her toothbrush but figured it was worth the sacrifice for one night.

There came a knock on the door and Zach shoved a toothbrush at her when she cracked the door open, "I always pack a couple extras for these trips, and I thought you might want one."

Smiling gratefully, she took it and quickly finished her

preparations.

Stepping back into the cabin, Zach was keenly aware of her long, tan legs and tried to ignore his instant erection.

Swiping up his sleep pants, he mumbled, "Don't wait up for me," as he traded places with her in the bathroom. As he brushed his teeth, Zach notice the lacey bra hanging on the towel rack and his dick twitched again. He considered the merits of a quick, cold shower. Given that a stench of smoke lingered on him, he decided that would be a reasonable excuse to offer and turned the knob. Shedding his clothes, he gritted his teeth and stepped under the steady stream of water.

A few minutes later, he was toweled off and back under control. With a deep breath, he opened the bathroom door and found the cabin dark. He could see Willow lying under the covers in the bunk with her back to the room. He turned off the bathroom light and crossed to the bunk, settling on his side near the edge. He had thought that he wouldn't be able to sleep but as the excitement of the evening wore off, exhaustion took over.

CHAPTER NINE

Willow awoke and wondered for a moment where she was. The room was still pitch dark. She was aware of strong muscular arms around her and a large male presence spooning her. There was also a large, hard penis pressing into her backside. She had remembered feeling Zach come to bed and listening as his breathing became deep and regular. She had intended to stay awake, but the events of the day caught up with her. Now, she listened, concerned that some noise had awakened her. The cabin remained silent other than the sounds of Zach's breathing in her ear. Then, as she felt his fingers squeeze her breast gently, she realized what had awakened her.

Willow waged an internal war with herself for the next several minutes. She knew that she should disengage herself from Zach's arms. But, doing so would undoubtedly wake him and she wasn't sure she could turn him away if he pushed for another kiss or more. His thumb rubbed across her nipple under the soft cotton and she felt her pulse quicken. Moisture was pooling between her legs too.

Feeling his dick twitch, she wondered if he was already awake and testing her receptiveness. Her training with TEP discouraged agents from becoming involved with people on missions. She was certain that, when the person was someone the agent was supposed to protect, it was even more important to remain objective. Still, all female TEP agents had implanted contraceptive devices so that there would be no unintended consequences if they did have a sexual encounter.

Deciding to find out, she whispered, "Zach, are you awake?"

His breathing didn't change, and he didn't respond.

Trying to ignore her arousal and her awareness of his, she closed her eyes and tried to force herself back to sleep. What she wouldn't give to just be a woman in this time. She could just roll over and kiss him awake. Then they could indulge their attraction if they wanted to.

However, sleep eluded Willow now. Her body was hyperaware of Zach's. Even the gentle rise and fall of his chest pushing at her back as he breathed increased her arousal. Unable to resist anymore, she wiggled her buttocks against his hard groin and felt a reactive twitch. The fingers on her breast squeezed as Zach awoke.

As he surfaced from a dream in which Willow was naked underneath him, Zach realized that his hardened cock was pressing eagerly into her backside and his hand was filled with the weight of her breast. He remembered her words about platonically sharing the bed and started to apologize, "Uh, I'm sorry, I didn't mean to take advantage –" he broke off.

Willow rolled onto her back, causing his hand to come off her breast before she rolled to face him. She stopped his words with a finger on his lips, "Shh," she whispered. Then, against her better judgment and her TEP training, she asked,

"Are you really sorry? Or would you rather put that erection to good use?"

Needing no more invitation, Zach found her lips in the dark and let loose the passion that had been building between them. Willow wrapped her arms around Zach's bare shoulders and gave herself up to the kiss. As he moved over her, she enjoyed the feel of his heavy body pressing hers into the bed. The feeling of her nipples being gently abraded by his movement was increasing the moisture in her panties.

Zach reached up to cup a breast again, its weight filling his palm as he rubbed a calloused thumb over the sensitive tip. Wanting to feel her bare skin, he reached down and rubbed his calloused hand up her silken hip to where the t-shirt was riding up mid abdomen. Sliding his fingers under the hem, he pushed the fabric up toward her shoulders. Willow lifted up a little, using her arms around his shoulders before letting go as the t-shirt cleared her head. Zach tossed it to the floor as Willow drew Zach's lips back to hers. Without the fabric between them, the way that his chest hairs rubbed her sensitive nipples sent little sparks of pleasure shooting to her core.

Then Zach bent his head and closed his warm lips over a sensitive peak. Willow tipped her head back, giving him easier access and released a groan as the pleasure built. The gentle pulling of his mouth felt amazing. She shifted her legs restlessly, the dampness between her legs increasing.

She slid her hand under the waistband of Zach's sleep pants and down his butt cheek. With her other hand, Willow tugged the front fabric down over his bulging penis, allowing it to spring free. The hot, silky length of him rubbed against her stomach.

Zach was dimly aware that things were escalating quickly. Trying to regain some of his control, he realized he needed a condom. He had some somewhere in his bags, but he hated to take the time to rummage around looking for it. That was likely to give them both time to rethink the wisdom of what they were doing and ruin the mood. His built-in bunk had had a drawer set in the frame, right near the headwall. Groping around, he found that this room had the same design. Maybe in the haste of vacating the cabin for them, the first mate had forgotten to empty it. He felt badly about going through the man's things. But Zach figured he would replace what he used. In the dark, he felt a square foil packet and closed his fingers around it. Relieved, he allowed himself to return his attention to the beautiful, warm woman underneath him. He returned his lips to her mouth, taking his time building the fire between them.

Willow was drowning in waves of need as Zach's lips played with hers. Who would have thought that the professor knew his way so well around a woman's body? When he rolled over onto his back, she was now straddling his hips. She took the opportunity to explore his incredible body. She trailed kisses down his throat and across a warm, hard pec muscle until she raked his small, tight nipple gently with her teeth. He groaned his pleasure. She delighted in the sound and reached a hand in between them to slide it around his engorged length.

"Oh, yeah," Zach encouraged her with a low rumble that vibrated underneath her. Willow ran her palm up and down his shaft, rubbing her thumb back and forth across his sensitive head. He gently grasped her wrist with one hand and groaned as he pressed the foil packet into the palm of her other hand. Without a word, she understood his message and ripped open the package and rolled the condom on deftly.

Then, without speaking, she shifted to remove her soaked panties. As she settled back down, she guided his erection as she sheathed him completely. Her inner muscles were stretched pleasantly with his rigid fullness. The satisfaction that the rapid move had them both feeling caused each of them to let out little groans of pleasure. Willow lifted up again and established a rhythm that Zach worked to match.

He felt the wave building at the base of his spine as he tried to hold on. His breathing was coming in harsh gasps. Their bodies had grown slick with the exertion and pleasure and their torsos were now sliding as they rubbed against each other. He could hear her breathing quicken as she panted and moaned incoherently.

Zach gritted his teeth until Willow flew over the edge, her inner muscles clenching rhythmically around him in her release. That was all he needed to follow her over the edge. The sounds of their harsh breaths settling was the only sound in the darkness. He was enjoying the feel of the soft warm body draped over the top of him as well as how her pliant core was still surrounding his now-flaccid length.

"That was so amazing I really don't want to move but I should take care of the condom," he managed to say after a few minutes.

Zach's words intruded into the pleasant laxness Willow was enjoying. She murmured a soft "Umm hmm," as she rolled carefully off him. Reality quickly intruded, dispelling her pleasure. Sleeping with the man she was supposed to be protecting was probably an unwise move. With a sigh, she turned so that her back was facing Zach when he returned a few minutes later, feigning sleep. She felt the mattress dip as Zach returned to the bed. He gathered her back to his warm chest and she chastised herself for liking the way that it felt to be surrounded by his strong body. The pattern of his breathing told her that he quickly fell asleep, but it was a long time before Willow's mind settled enough to allow her to rest again.

CHAPTER TEN

Early the next morning, Willow eased out from under the covers and wrote Zach a quick note. She hated to leave but they would need some food. While she prepared a quick meal in the galley and grabbed some prepackaged snacks, she talked to the captain. He agreed with her that having someone stay with Zach was more important than any deck duties, so she was reassigned to watching over the professor.

When she returned to the room, Zach was awake and sitting on the edge of the bunk with his head in his hands. When he raised his face to look at her, Willow could see anguish in his eyes.

She pushed down the disappointment that he seemed to be regretting their time together as she asked, "Having second thoughts about last night?"

Zach was startled out of his revelry by the question and reminded of the pleasure they had given each other and smiled broadly, "No, no. That was great!" But his most recent thoughts washed back over him, and his expression sobered as he continued. "I realized that after the fire, some of my algae was released into the ocean. My built-in safety features to prevent such a thing were bypassed. I'm sure that whoever did it thought that the strain would be lost. However, I'm worried that the move will disrupt the balance of the ocean's ecosystem. What if there is no check to balance the algae and it grows prolifically? It could cause dead zones where no fish can survive or, even worse, cause massive oil slicks that have to be cleaned up. Instead of helping the planet, maybe my discovery will destroy it!"

Cold dread washed over Willow with his words. Everything that had been happening since the day Zach had survived the shark attack was rewriting history and impacting her future. What if he was right and the release of the algae had resulted in another massive ecologic disaster? Crossing to the desk, she set the food down and pulled her communicator out of her pocket.

As she began typing, Zach looked at her confused, "You know that there isn't any cell service out this far, right?"

Engrossed in sending her status report, Willow nodded absently.

Zach was confused. In light of all the things that had been happening around him, he should be suspicious of everyone. He had felt he could trust Willow but what if she was just trying to get close to him to steal his research? Carefully, he asked, "Then who are you communicating with?"

Willow sent her message and looked up to see doubt in Zach's face. Realizing her error, she sought for a plausible answer. A satellite smart phone would be out of reach of the average person in this time period and only make her look more guilty.

When she didn't immediately reply, Zach stood and began pacing. "Are you in on this? I know that you were with me when the spear was shot at me and the fire was set but maybe you are working with someone and trying to gain my trust." As much as he didn't want to believe his own words, Zach realized that he needed to consider every option.

Willow met his stare and answered honestly, "No, Zach. I'm not working with the person trying to kill you." Hurt boiled up and Willow surprised herself as she burst out, "How could you think that I was just using my body to play you last night? I thought we had an amazing, real connection. I could never pretend feelings like that!"

With all his jumbled thoughts, Zach had almost forgotten how amazing the sex between them had been. Trying to keep a level head, he asked again, "Then who were you just trying to contact?"

Her communicator chirped that a response had been received and the suspicion was back in his eyes. Seeing no other way around it, Willow decided to try to tell Zach the truth. It was so ingrained in her training to never talk about time travel so she wasn't sure how she could convince him, but she had to try.

With a sigh, she said, "You really should sit down. This may take a little while and you may not believe what I'm about to tell you."

Zach reluctantly sat down again on the edge of the bunk. Their breakfast food was forgotten.

Willow began hesitantly, "I saw that you read science fiction."

Zach nodded, perplexed by the sudden change of subject.

"Well, you know how some author comes up with a device that can do a fantastic thing and that inspires some scientific genius to actually create it?"

"I suppose so," Zach's reply was noncommittal.

Feeling like she was botching her explanation, Willow

changed tactics a bit, "As a scientist, you know that there are new discoveries all the time that broaden our understanding of the world as we know it, right?"

Zach couldn't figure out what this all had to do with who she was texting, but he nodded.

Willow cringed inwardly at her words as she blurted out, "Well, just such a genius invented a way to travel through time." At Zach's disbelieving expression, she clarified, "I was sent here from the future to protect you and your process."

Zach was silent for a long minute as he looked from her to his stack of books and over to his jar filled with algae. Was she playing some elaborate joke on him? She hadn't seemed delusional in their dealings up to this point. And, she had saved his life on multiple occasions now.

Feeling foolish for entertaining the possibility that what she said was true, Zach asked skeptically, "Now I'm not saying that I believe you, but what proof do you have?"

Willow turned her phone towards him, and Zach could see a '15%' displayed on the screen that flashed green as she spoke, "Let me back up a little bit. In the original timeline, the day of the shark attack, you died."

Her statement was blunt, and Zach was stunned.

She went on, "I don't know if it was running out of air during the dive or the shark attack, because the only part of the record that survived just states that you died but not how it happened. I got a job on the crew to try to keep you safe. However, the person or persons responsible keep trying to eliminate you and your process. Our suspicion is that one of the companies who offered to buy your algae is behind the attacks. If they can't buy it and hide it away in some file never to be seen again, then they want to eliminate you before you can give it away to the world."

Zach considered her words thoughtfully and nodded.

Willow continued, "I would never have told you any of this, but you were worried about the release of your algae and I realized that your concern was valid. Everything that is happening now, is different from the way that events were originally after your death. What you said about the algae getting into the wild has happened and I needed to check on the result. It could have changed the world in my time. This screen says that the wild algae had a positive effect but only in a small way. Perhaps not enough of it was released," she added.

Zach stared at the screen. The display didn't really tell him much about her claim although, if she was for real, he was relieved that he wasn't indirectly responsible for an ecologic disaster. At his own thought, he shook himself. How could he possibly be considering believing her? Latching onto part of her story, he asked, "You mentioned 'your time'. What year would that be?"

"2172," was her quick response.

Zach was silent for another minute and Willow didn't press him.

When he spoke again, Zach asked, "Is there some other proof that you can offer me?"

Willow considered, trying to think of something tangible and not of this time period. Glancing at her wrist, she asked, "Would you agree that a biometric tattoo that is invisible would be something not available now?"

Zach had heard of some people trying to develop implanted microchips that could be scanned but nothing in the form of an invisible tattoo. "Show me," he directed.

Willow turned her wrist toward the ceiling and showed it to Zach. Her skin was slightly tanned but clear from any visible marks. She thumbed the screen of her smartphone and it emitted an infrared beam that she passed over the inside of her wrist. Under the different light spectrum, Zach could see a small eternity symbol that seemed to glow. It disappeared abruptly when the light was removed. "We use the tattoo for entrance into our compound in the future. Also, there are enough of us who time travel that we don't all know each other by sight. This allows us to authenticate each other when we meet on assignment in the past."

Zach felt that her explanation made sense to this point. He went on to ask her questions about what Earth was like in her time and she answered candidly. Even though he was not hugely interested in astronomy, Zach had heard about the star light years away that had been showing signs of becoming unstable. Everything Willow said sounded plausible. Yet, he felt like he had been plunked down in the middle of a sci-fi movie. Was he crazy for wanting to believe her?

"You mentioned other time travelers and you said 'our suspicions' earlier. Who is on the other end of that device, sending you messages?"

Willow briefly described TEP and the supercomputer artificial intelligence that guided them on their missions. She held up her screen again. "This '15%' indicates how successful I have been in my mission so far. The fact that it doesn't read '100%' or close to it means that the danger to you is not over and someone is still trying to kill you." With a sigh, she tried to press her point, "I think that we need to get you off this boat ASAP. There's nowhere for you to really hide here. If they haven't already thought about poisoning you, that will probably be the next move. Depending on what they use, this far out to sea, it may be impossible to get you back to an antidote on the mainland in time."

Zach didn't want to cut his class short. Some of the students had been waiting several semesters for the chance to get on this ship and study with him. Still, what good would he be to his students if he was dead?

Willow could see that she was getting through to Zach. She had saved her best argument for last and laid it out now, "Zach, just staying on the ship puts everyone else in danger too. If whoever is behind everything gets desperate enough, they may cause an accident that risks everyone else and even the boat itself. Take the fire for instance. That was a stupid, desperate move that could have sunk the ship. Whoever is behind the attacks isn't thinking clearly, that's for sure! What if their next idea is equally short-sighted and foolhardy?"

Zach couldn't believe that he was finding himself convinced that she was from the future. However, he heard the truth of her words about the attacks and reached his decision. With a nod, he agreed, "Okay, you've made your point. I'll see if there has been any response to my email asking for a substitute. If not, I'll tell the University that I have to leave the ship anyway. I'll ask Captain Harvey if there is a supply delivery that we could hitch a ride back on. However, I don't think that it will be happening today, so I want to finish a couple of experiments that are quite important to my research while we wait. That is, if you think that I can do it safely," he added.

"What do you need to do?" she asked.

"Well, I was wanting to track dispersal rates by releasing phosphorescent dinoflagellates. The surface temperature is warm enough for them right now and I wanted to photograph the plume from a distance to extrapolate what would happen if the algae were released. That test seems even more important now."

Willow groaned inwardly. Even if he was the only diver, a night experiment would be very risky. Although she had to admit the bioluminescent idea would provide some good data. And, as he had pointed out, it was more important to track dispersal patterns now. After a thoughtful consideration, she asked, "It would just be taking video footage underwater?"

Zach nodded.

Giving in, Willow agreed, "Okay. But we will need to do the test tonight. And, I will be the one in the water." She hated to leave him alone in the launch but figured that would be the safer place for Zach to be.

Having reached her decision, she announced, "I'll call the Captain and tell him we need the launch tonight but I'm not going to offer any more details. I'll also ask him about the next flight out while you work on your emails," she offered.

Thinking about the experiment, Willow suggested, "Pick one student or a deck crew member that you think you can trust to release the whatever-you-called-them. They don't need to know anything about what we are doing. All they have to do is dump the bucket at the prescribed time, right?"

Pleased, Zach agreed. "I'll make a list of everything we need for tonight and figure out who we can get to help out. I'll also set up some experiments for the students to work on while they wait for my replacement."

CHAPTER ELEVEN

2018, Atlantic Ocean off the coast of the United States

Willow and Zach placed a conference call with Captain Harvey, and he was in favor of their decision to get off the boat for a time. He agreed to radio the mainland and have the next supply flight moved up for the following day. After making the arrangements for their last experiment and promising to keep as few people as possible in the loop about their plans, they ended the call.

Satisfied with their plans, Willow turned her thoughts to the scheduled night dive. She was uncomfortable with the logistics of it. It would be easy for someone to slip off the main ship in some dive gear and make another try at them while they were isolated. If she was the saboteur, that's what she would do.

As they stayed in Zach's cabin awaiting nightfall, he worked on his computer analyzing the data he had collected so far on the performance of his tube system in scrubbing microplastics. What he saw was encouraging, despite the loss of the algae that had been released. Willow spent her time sending the AIs in the future new questions about the various people on the ship, still trying to figure out who was behind the attempts on Zach. If she could identify the people involved, maybe they wouldn't have to leave the ship after all. However, she was getting nowhere with that strategy.

Looking up at Zach, Willow had a realization that she doubted he would like. Clearing her throat to get his attention, she began, "Zach, do you think it wise to leave the algae tubes functioning while you aren't here to supervise them? I mean, what if you don't get right back here and whoever is behind all this tries again to release everything into the ocean in an effort to discredit your work as ecologically unsafe?"

Zach looked up and considered her words. Removing his glasses and rubbing his eyes he considered for only a moment before he sighed, "You are right. That is something we have to consider. There really is no other option but to kill off the algae before we leave."

He went on to explain, "I had planned that I would drain down the water and pump the sludge into sealed buckets for transport back to the States. Maybe we could still take a bucket with us?" he asked.

Willow considered and figured that they could add it to their gear so she nodded and asked, "Will it all fit in one bucket?"

Zach shook his head with disappointment. He felt like he was consigning one of his children to a death sentence, "No, I'll have to dump bleach in the rest of the samples. That will kill the algae. The captain will have to dispose of everything after that. It's really the only way to keep another unintentional release from happening."

Willow could see that Zach was upset and disappointed

at the prospect of ruining his own work and said gently, "I'm sorry. I wish there was another way."

Zach shook himself mentally. After all, he would still have viable samples and he could build on what he had accomplished so far. Squaring his shoulders, he announced, "It will be okay. I can start over again when all of this is sorted out."

Willow had gone over her dive equipment multiple times and was carefully keeping their gear within sight at all times. She was electing to use a typical mouthpiece that wouldn't allow her to speak into a communication system like the team had used on the previous dive. She wouldn't have any way to talk with Zach in the launch and that worried her. However, she wanted to be using equipment she was comfortable with and the full-face mask with microphone and speaker hampered her vision. Willow had agreed to wear a rope around her waist while she was down on the dive. At regular intervals, Zach would check in by giving it a little tug. She would respond back with an answering tug. Three tugs would be an indication that one of them was in distress and the experiment would be cut short.

Willow had decided that one way she could potentially keep Zach safe was by pretending that he would be the one doing the diving and that she would be in the launch while he conducted his experiment. They had gone over the underwater video equipment in the privacy of his cabin. On deck, Zach made a big deal about double-checking the equipment. He had been reluctant to allow Willow to place herself in danger by switching places with him. However, while he struggled not to let it be a blow to his manhood, he could see the point of making the switch. He would still be vulnerable if someone made an attempt on the launch. It didn't stop him from worrying about Willow's safety while she was underwater in his place though.

After showing the member of the deck crew who had been assigned the release of the dinoflagellates how to conduct that portion of the experiment, they transferred their gear to the launch just as the sun slipped below the horizon. They eased the tender away from the ship and off into the rapidly darkening seas.

The current of the Gulf Stream travelled at a rate around six miles an hour and they wanted to see how far the tiny glowing life forms would travel in an hour. That was a length of time that would be safe for diving and not fill the memory cards of the cameras. Willow thought that the distance of six miles might be enough to discourage any attempt on them during their time away. However, she was listening to that feeling of unease in the pit of her stomach. She wouldn't rest easy until they were safely back aboard the research vessle.

The waves at night were calm and before long, they throttled back and cut the motor. There would be some drifting of the launch but, since Willow was connected to the dive boat, they wouldn't have to worry about keeping to a particular spot. Willow looked back and the lights of the ship had merged to one large bright spot. In the sudden silence, the waves lapping at the hull of the launch was the only sound. Willow felt very isolated and vulnerable and she didn't like it.

Checking her dive watch, she announced, "I've got eighteen minutes left to get into position so we're cutting it close." As she spoke, she was shrugging into the harness of her tank and then scooped up her mask before settling it over her eyes. After putting the regulator into her mouth and testing it, she gave Zach a thumbs up. Sitting on the gunwale, she applied her swim fins and flipped neatly backward into the pitch blackness.

Resurfacing next to the boat, she grasped the rope that Zach tossed to her and tied it securely around her waist. Then she reached up and Zach handed over the underwater cameras. There was one with a broad angle stacked on top of one with a zoom lens. They had twin safety straps that she quickly snapped to the rings on her dive harness. With another thumbs-up, she sank back below the surface. Zach knew that he wouldn't see her for the next hour. Totally alone now, he felt vulnerable. He knew that Willow had been right to be concerned. While it was too late now, he wondered why he had felt that this experiment was so important to conduct.

The clouds prevented much moonlight from illuminating the surface of the waves, but Zach still scanned the ocean between the launch and the ship, looking for any signs they had been followed. Keeping one hand on the rope Willow was wearing, Zach felt the time inching by. Finally, he felt one tug. She was doing okay and had reached the designated depth and started filming. Glancing at his watch, Zach saw that they still had two minutes before the release of the dinoflagellates.

While Zach doubted that the cameras would pick up the phosphorescent glow right away, if the experiment went as he hoped, he would be able to observe the rate of travel and the dispersal pattern in the fast ocean current. If they were propelled as quickly as he expected, the tiny glowing life forms should pass by the cameras within the next hour. Zach gave an answering tug and settled in to wait.

Having time to think, he couldn't help how his mind went to the bizarre circumstances he found himself in. Was he really convinced that Willow was a woman sent from the future to save his life? As difficult as it was to wrap his head around, she had made a compelling argument and he would be foolish to ignore her warning, given the way thinks kept happening around him. Prior to this, Zach had led a very dull, orderly life. Having so many accidents in such a short period of time was statistically highly improbable. Still, he couldn't quite bring himself to believe her completely. Perhaps some other explanation that wasn't as far-fetched would be revealed with time.

Willow didn't mind diving in the dark. While it was difficult to keep one's equilibrium and not panic at the total blackness surrounding her, she had completed enough dives that she knew the little tricks to keep her nerves calm. Consulting the glowing compass on her wrist, she positioned herself in the direction of the main ship and began recording. The silence was broken only by the sound of her own breathing and the bubbles being released as she exhaled.

She checked her dive watch for the umpteenth time, noting that about forty minutes had gone by. Zach had tugged once on the rope on several occasions and she had responded with one tug in return. Willow was excited to see that there was clearly a glowing cloud advancing towards her. It had started as a small speck in the gloom and steadily gotten larger. She hoped that the camera was recording the footage as she was seeing it.

Her eyes had adjusted and there was a faint glow from her dive watch and compass that lit the area right in front of her slightly. Watching the glowing organisms coming at her was mesmerizing, rather like watching clouds growing on the horizon.

Despite her preoccupation, her subconscious registered the cessation of a slight whirring sound that she hadn't been aware of. Reflexively, she turned toward the sound, forgetting about the cameras momentarily. As she pivoted, there was a faint flicker of light reflecting off metal as something hit the top camera and was deflected away. The force of the blow knocked them from her hands, and they were now hanging from where she had clipped them to her harness.

In a split second, Willow realized that what had hit the camera was a spear from a spear gun. Reaching for her ankle, she pulled her dive knife from its sheath and brandished it in front of her. The spear guns were a single shot device, but it was possible that her attacker had brought another one along. She realized then that the change in sound that had alerted her had been a dive assist electric motor being shut off. That would explain how the diver had covered the distance between them and the main ship.

From out of the gloom, there was a dark shape that came at her from above and Willow glimpsed a blade as the diver tried to slash her air hose. Willow twisted away and the blade missed its mark. She slashed out with her own knife as she tried to move out of range of another possible attack. Willow felt her knife connect with something and she pressed upward. There was a large bubble of air around the divers and Willow realized that she had connected with the other diver's BCD. She could hear turbulence from swim fins and the motor of the assist device kicked in again. Willow trained her focus on the sound but there were no further attacks and the whirring sound of the motor was receding back toward the main ship.

Now that her immediate threat had seemed to pass, she was worried that the diver might have attacked the launch first. Concerned for Zach, Willow reached above her for the rope, worried that it might have been severed in the attack. Finding it, she gave a tug. There was a prompt tug from the surface. She shifted back toward the ship and lifted the cameras to point back in that direction. She had no way of knowing if they had been damaged by the blow from the spear. She was torn for only a moment that Zach would be disappointed to not have the most critical part of his experiment recorded. Despite that, she needed to get back to the surface in case her attacker decided to try again. The launch itself could be a target although they had radio communication with the research vessel if there was need for a rescue.

With several powerful kicks of her fins, Willow was propelling herself up to the surface. When her head broke into fresh air, she spit out her regulator and used the rope to pull herself back to the launch.

"Zach!" she cried out to get his attention.

Hearing his name, Zach looked at his watch. Not enough time had passed for the video to be complete. Instinctively he knew that there had been trouble.

"Willow, are you okay?" he called back.

Reaching the side of the boat, she grabbed the edge and replied, "Yeah, but give me a hand in. Quickly!" she urged.

As she wiggled out of the straps holding her tank in place, she unzipped her buoyancy control vest and filled Zach in on what had happened. Looking at the cameras laying on the deck, she concluded, "I'm sorry that I didn't get all the footage, but I didn't think I should stay down there. It's so dark a person can't see until someone is right on top of you."

Zach had been looking Willow over for any injury when she had said that she was attacked. Now that he was hearing her apologize for not staying underwater with a killer, he was incredulous. "You can't think that I would have wanted you to stay down and risk your life for an experiment?"

"Well, I figured you would understand but I still feel badly. Is there another way we can try to get more footage?"

Zach couldn't believe that she was being so calm about what had just happened and that she was still focused on his experiment. Bending down to pick up the cameras, he could see that they were both still recording. Scanning the dark waves between them and the ship, he could actually see the glowing cloud beneath the surface moving closer to them.

Spotting the rope still tied to the rail, he picked up the end that had been around Willow's waist. Threading it through the hooks and tying the loose end around the rail too, he lowered the cameras back underwater. As he worked, he explained, "It may not be aimed directly at the dinoflagellates but hopefully I can use the ropes to adjust the angle. Maybe it will work and maybe it won't, but it will be safer than having you down there like a sitting duck."

"That's a good idea," Willow replied. Since the glow was becoming more visible, she asked, "Would it help to record the movement from the surface? My communicator has a camera just like your smart phone and I have it here with me. We could transfer the footage to your computer later." Since cell phones didn't work this far from land, Zach had left his behind on the ship.

"Sure. There should still be information I can use even with the surface distortion." Zach replied.

Willow grabbed her communicator and opened the camera function and began her recording. She had the glowing cloud squarely centered on the screen and Zach, hopefully, had the cameras trained on the tiny creatures from below. The glow grew brighter and came right alongside them before passing on by. Willow kept her recording going until she could no longer see the biolumenescent creatures in the surrounding darkness.

Shifting her gaze from the screen of her device, she looked at Zach, who was leaning over the rail with a rope in each hand. Catching sight of the light from the ship in the distance behind Zach, she realized that she should have radioed the ship sooner. There was a chance that they could apprehend her attacker when the diver returned to the vessel. Moving over to the radio, she made the call now and explained what had happened to the first mate on night duty. He agreed to post watches and conduct a cabin inspection to see if anyone was missing.

Satisfied that she had done everything she could for the time being, Willow turned back to Zach who was pulling up the cameras and dragging them back aboard the launch.

He sat back on the deck, silent for a moment now that the flurry of finishing the experiment had passed. Disappointment washed over him as he realized that the diver had thought he was the one underwater. Every time he tried to advance his science, he felt like he was being sabotaged. He didn't know how he would be able to work against such continuous pressure. Zach's shoulders slumped as his discouraged thoughts overwhelmed him.

Willow saw Zach's expression and offered again in a quiet voice, "I'm sorry."

Zach lifted his head and looked up at her as he replied, "You shouldn't feel sorry about anything. None of this is your fault. If anything, your quick thinking allowed me to get some useful information. Even if the underwater cameras don't pick up anything, it hasn't been a total failure."

Zach stood up and came to stand in front of Willow, lightly cupping her elbows as he kept speaking, "You said that you hadn't been hurt, but are you really okay?"

Keeping her mind on the mission to protect Zach

and then focusing on his experiment had been her way of preventing thoughts about how close she had come to being harpooned. She was upset with herself that her assailant had managed to get so close to her. Still, now that it was all over, she felt a wave of relief that both she and Zach hadn't been harmed. She smiled up at him and reassured, "Yes, I'm fine. Really. It was a close thing though, I'm sorry to admit."

Feeling Zach's warm fingers around her arms and seeing the real concern for her in his eyes, she reached up and pulled his lips down to hers for a leisurely kiss. She wanted to celebrate being alive by immersing herself in this man.

Zach caught the emotion in her kiss and responded, losing himself in exploring her mouth. He wasn't a man who normally moved so quickly with a woman. Yet, with this one, he found that his body was overriding the common sense his brain tried to present.

Willow was tempted to undress Zach and give in to the pleasure right there on the launch. It would be private, so far from the main ship. However, she worried that there was a slim possibility that they might not be alone. The unknown diver could also have sabotaged their propeller before attacking her. She needed to make sure that they got back to the research vessel safely before giving in to her distraction. If she dropped her guard, Zach could pay the price for her inattention. It would be difficult to explain to Commander Bishop that she had allowed emotions to compromise her mission.

Breaking the contact with a sigh, Willow said, "We really should get back to the ship. Maybe they will have caught the person who attacked me as they came back aboard. It would solve our need to leave if the threat out here was neutralized."

Zach was struggling to get himself back under control. He nodded and reluctantly agreed, "You're right, I suppose.

Let's get under way."

CHAPTER TWELVE

The first thing Willow wanted was a shower. However, they had to stow their gear away and update Captain Harvey. When they had radioed the bridge, the first mate had awakened the Captain and he wanted to know everything that had happened. He authorized a roll call to determine if anyone was missing. While there were two students who were ill in their cabin, everyone was present.

Dejected, they headed back to the borrowed cabin. When the door closed behind them, Willow again thought about how good that shower was going to feel. She still felt keyed up from all the adrenaline. Turning to Zach, she caught the desire in his eyes. Impulsively, she arched her brow at him as she invited, "Care to join me? The shower may be tiny but, if we're quick, there should be plenty of hot water."

Zach really couldn't understand his attraction to her. He was already getting hard thinking about sharing the shower with her. With an answering grin, he drew her mouth to his for a kiss. The touch ignited the complex emotions they were feeling and, with a flurry of clothing falling to the floor, Willow pulled Zach along as they made their way to the small bathroom. They were naked by the time she broke the contact and leaned over to adjust the knobs.

Zach took the opportunity to trail kisses down her neck and along the ridge of her bare shoulder. Willow found Zach's lips distracting as she fumbled with the temperature. Figuring that they could fine tune it later if need be, she pulled his mouth back to hers for another searing kiss. As their tongues dueled, she backed into the stream of water. The two of them barely fit in the small space and he was quickly pressing her bare back up against the cold tiles. Without a moment's hesitation, he sheathed himself to the hilt in her slick passage. While their mouths devoured each other and the water sluiced over them making their bodies slide wetly, Zach pumped and thrust inside her.

Willow's release slammed into her quick and hard. The intensity of it pulled Zach under with her. Only when they were both sated did he realized that he had forgotten a condom.

After a few minutes of standing together under the steadily beating spray, Zach felt himself slide out of her warmth. With the water rapidly cooling, Willow grabbed a shampoo bottle and quickly began sudsing his hair and worked her soapy hands up and down the firm muscles of his chest. Zach followed suit and slathered suds up and down her luscious curves.

When they had taken their turns under the spray and rinsed off, Zach turned off the water and led Willow from the shower. With a quick kiss, he handed her a towel before grabbing another one and quickly drying himself and wrapping it around his hips.

Zach wasn't usually so careless and hesitated to start

the conversation. However, he felt he needed to face the potential problem head on. "Um, Willow, I'm sorry that I forgot about the condom. It really isn't like me. I always use one. I want to know if there are any consequences that result." The thought of a pregnancy terrified him, but he wanted her to know that he wouldn't shirk his responsibility.

Willow saw the fear in his expression and realized his concern. With a small smile she reassured him, "Not to worry, Zach. All female TEP officers have an implanted contraceptive device. And, I have to undergo a total body decon after each jump. So, I'm clean and I'm not worried."

Zach was relieved by her words but was reminded of their strange circumstances. She was here to protect him. When her job was done, she would travel back to her time. Probably without even thinking any more about him. He would be smart not to let his heart get involved.

Trying to set a less personal tone between them, he grabbed his sleep pants from where they had been hung on a hook on the bathroom door. The t-shirt Willow had used the previous night was also hanging there. He tried for casual as he tossed it to her, saying, "Well that's good to know. We really should turn in now, we have a lot to do tomorrow."

Willow was puzzled by the abrupt change in Zach. She thought about trying to figure out what was behind it. However, she realized that there was no future for her with him. While they were combustible together, it probably would be better to try to put some emotional distance back between them.

Catching the shirt, she stepped back into the bathroom to put it on and brush her teeth. When she came back into the cabin, Zach had swapped his towel for his pants. While she headed for the bunk, he brushed his teeth. Willow turned off the light and slid under the covers. It felt awkward sharing the bed platonically after they had shared such an intense experience together in the shower. Firming her resolve, Willow knew she needed to rest up to prepare for the next day. They had a lot to do and she needed to be extra vigilant. She really hoped that getting Zach back to land would change his chances of survival.

CHAPTER THIRTEEN

Willow and Zach awoke the next morning to the ringing of the ship phone. Captain Harvey was calling to tell them that the supply shipment was due in three hours. After Zach thanked the man and assured him that they would be ready, he turned to look at Willow. He wanted to indulge himself with her delectable body again but ruefully said, "Looks like we have a lot to get done this morning."

Willow had been disappointed that they hadn't been able to catch their saboteur. However, she was glad that Zach had finally been convinced to leave. "I'll grab my gear from my cabin while you get your stuff packed up here. Then we can see about shutting down your experiment."

Dressing quickly, she extracted a promise from Zach to lock the cabin door behind her and not let anyone else in while she was gone. Making short work of collecting her gear, Willow thought about the two students who had been reported ill during the headcount last night. It was standard practice to isolate ill people on the boat, but she decided that she would peek in on them quickly before she left just to be sure.

Mindy answered the door looking pale with dark circles under her eyes. In the background, Willow could hear sounds of vomiting from the bathroom. The stale air that hit her face as the door was opened was fetid smelling. Mindy wasn't pleased with being disturbed but assured Willow that they didn't need anything. Since the girls seemed legitimately ill, Willow made her apologies and, scooping up her things, headed back to Zach's cabin.

She knocked and announced herself and the door was quickly flung open. Inside, Zach had stacked his things neatly atop his trunk except for his laptop which was open on the desk. She could see that he was agitated aagain. After closing the door behind her, he began pacing around the small cabin as he spoke, "I got on to the ship's satellite wi-fi so I could check to see if the school was sending another professor for the students. I wanted to be able to tell them something when I announce that I'm leaving, and you'll never guess what I found."

As Willow shrugged and shook her head, he went on, "There was a message from the Arlington Police Department. It seems that my apartment was broken into and vandalized. All the tanks where I was growing algae samples were smashed. Everything has been destroyed. They are wanting a list of valuables, but it doesn't look like a robbery since the television and stereo are still there. About the only thing clearly missing is my desktop computer."

Concerned, Willow asked, "Was all your research on that computer? Could the formula for creating the algae be stolen and patented by someone else?"

Zach shook his head sheepishly, "No. I use that computer mostly for gaming and school-related material. All the research on my algae is on my laptop," he added as he swept his hand toward the open computer.

Willow thought about Zach's news for a moment. She could see that he was very upset and with good reason. She knew that he would want to go there right away to assess the damage. Still, it might be risky for them to check it out once they were back on the mainland.

"I have to say, I'm rather concerned about this, Zach. It probably indicates that multiple people are after you and your research. Going to your apartment might be walking into a trap," she considered aloud.

Zach resumed his pacing and replied, "I understand but I have backup copies of my files hidden there and several other strains I was working on hybridizing. Algae isn't easily killed by being out of water. There may still be some specimens I can salvage if I have the right supplies."

Willow looked at the hopeful expression on Zach's face and didn't have the heart to disappoint him further. Knowing that it wasn't the best tactical decision, she reluctantly agreed. "Okay, we can pay a visit to your place, but I want you to have all the supplies you will need, and you will be on a countdown. After thirty minutes, we leave, no matter what stays behind. If we're lucky, we'll escape the notice of whoever trashed the place."

Inwardly, she doubted her words. If she was on the other side, Willow thought that she would be nearby with a trip alarm in place. That way, even if she was taking a short nap, she would know the moment anyone was inside the apartment. Her only hope was that the people that had been recruited online may not be as professional as she was. Perhaps they didn't have access to such tech. Maybe it really had just been a vandalism in the hope that Zach's research would be ruined or, at least set back a few years.

In her preoccupation with this latest development,

Willow almost forgot about Zach's purpose in checking his emails in the first place. She checked her watch and realized they would have to call the students together for an announcement soon. "Did you hear back from the university about a replacement?"

Zach was feeling better now that Willow had agreed to go to his place to check out the damage. "No. I got so sidetracked." Returning to the chair at the desk, he continued, "Let me check now."

With nothing else to do in his cabin and plenty awaiting them on deck, she asked, "Should I start draining the sea water out of the tubes to concentrate the algae?"

Zach looked up from his screen, "Sure. That would be a good idea." After he explained what she would need to do, she was on her way with the agreement to be back in fifteen minutes. "We will move all our gear to the deck together and, by then the tubes should be ready for you to empty," she said as she left.

At the towering glass cylinders, she told the guards to radio the Captain for permission for her to have access. Once the approval came through, she began turning knobs below the inline filters. This would drain the seawater but didn't risk the algae pouring into the ocean as well.

Then, she turned her attention to the supply closet where deck cleaning materials were kept. Searching around, she found a couple of empty plastic buckets with snap-on lids and some bottles of bleach. Checking that her time was nearly up, she headed back to get Zach. Her eyes kept scanning the halls and stairs as she moved, always looking for a potential attack.

When Willow arrived back at the cabin, Zach was ready to leave. They quickly retraced her steps to return to the deck. The level of seawater in the tubes was receding nicely and Zach went over to inspect the buckets she had found. After a quick rinse out, he turned the spigots Willow had opened so that they were now closed.

As he worked, Captain Harvey's voice came across the ship's loudspeaker, summoning all the students to the mid-deck for an announcement. Zach turned a different handle and, while one of the buckets was positioned underneath, drained the rest of the tube into it. He repeated the process with the next two tubes. With the buckets now filled, he stepped to the ladder while carrying a bottle of bleach. He had salvaged what he could and would need to make sure the rest of the algae would become inert.

Willow reached out a hand to stop him, saying, "I'll do that. You would make a tempting target up there. Why don't you secure the covers on those buckets while I pour the bleach?"

Zach understood and nodded.

While Willow quickly scaled the ladder and began pouring the liquid into each of the remaining tubes, the students started to congregate on the deck below her. Glancing down, she did a quick head count. All of them seemed to be present, even the girls who were ill, although they stood slightly away from the others.

Zach began talking and Willow learned that the University had agreed to send another professor. While Zach hadn't told the dean about the attacks on his life, perhaps the news of his apartment invasion had convinced the man that he needed to be back on the mainland to attend to business. There were plenty of moans of disappointment from the various students, but Zach went on to say that he had prepared some experiments as homework that could be completed by the time the new professor arrived. He reassured them that he would be in communication with his replacement about what had been accomplished so far in the class and that everyone's grades were in good standing at this point.

From her vantage point, Willow could see a helicopter approaching in the distance. That would be their ride arriving. Having finished with the bleach, she climbed back down. By the time the chopper had offloaded the supplies and their belongings had been stowed away, it would be time to empty the remaining cylinders. Turning to one of the crew members standing guard, she asked him to retrieve a large barrel they could use for that purpose. It would be placed in the hold with the other dangerous chemicals the science ship generated and would be returned to land for proper disposal at the end of the voyage.

The helicopter arrived and landed easily on the aft deck, its rotors spooling down. The ill students were sent back to their cabin and every other able hand made their way toward the back of the ship. With the arrival of the barrel, Zach went to work draining the glass tubes and Willow reluctantly left him to that task. She positioned herself at the head of the human supply chain that would offload the new provisions. That way she could keep an eye on their ride to make sure that no one attempted to sabotage it. However, leaving Zach alone on the deck above made her nervous and she kept one eye on him until he was finished.

At that point, he gathered their gear and started loading it into the other side of the chopper. When the supplies were removed and Willow and Zach were ready to depart, Captain Harvey appeared to see them off. After a hearty handshake and wishes of good luck were exchanged, they climbed aboard and strapped themselves in.

Sliding the doors closed as the pilot started the rotors spinning, Willow was anxious to be airborne. They all donned protective headsets so they would be able to communicate with each other during the flight. Then the chopper was lifting smoothly away. As the deck of the ship grew smaller beneath them, Willow breathed a little sigh of relief. She wouldn't fully relax until they were back on solid ground on the mainland, but this was a good first step.

She kept waiting for her communicator to vibrate in her pocket, signaling a status update and, hopefully, success in her mission. The ribbon of land on the horizon had taken on forms and details such as buildings by the time she felt the message come through. Eagerly, she pulled it out and was disappointed to see that the screen was still red and only registered fifty percent. She had hoped that getting Zach away from the ship would resolve his problems. It was confusing to try to figure out what this update meant. Was the company still going to send more people after him even though the research in his apartment had been destroyed? Was the person on the ship still going to find a way to pursue him? Would whoever had vandalized the apartment make another attempt on Zach? Because history had been changed, she had no way of knowing where the next attack might come from.

As the helicopter swooped over the airfield and hovered for landing, she thought about her promise to get Zach to his apartment and began planning how to make that happen. It looked like she was still going to be watching over him for a while. As she considered his strong body and handsome bespectacled face, she realized that part of her really didn't mind having to stay close to the man. Pushing those thoughts aside, she resolved to focus on the mission.

CHAPTER FOURTEEN

Willow had to think quickly about transportation. She doubted that the stolen car she had left near the marina would still be there. It would have probably been reported and impounded by now. She could always look for another vehicle to steal but it seemed like an unnecessary risk that could call attention to them and potentially blow back on Zach if they were caught. She had some funds and it was unlikely that anyone searching for Zach would connect it to her if she paid cash when she rented a vehicle in the name of her alias.

The owner of the helicopter charter service offered to drive them over to the main terminal where they could rent a car. After their gear was stowed in the back of his truck, they made the short trip. Willow left Zach with the gear and went inside to make the arrangements. There was no reason to think that he was in any more danger at the moment than any other person at the terminal, but she warned him to be watchful before she left.

A short time later, keys in hand, she returned to his side for a moment as she announced, "I'll be back in a few with our ride."

After pulling up to the curb and reloading all the gear, they settled into the car and merged into the busy terminal traffic. As Willow kept her eyes on her driving she asked, "So, what will you need for your trip to your apartment?"

"I was thinking about that as we were flying and jotted down a list. If we can go to a hardware store, I should be able to get everything there."

While they were waiting at a stop light, Willow put a request for the nearest hardware store into her communicator. The GPS coordinates popped up along with a map showing her how to get there. They drove for a few more minutes until they were in the parking lot. Weighing the risks, she decided to keep her cash for potential needs later and told him to go in to buy everything on his own. She would stay outside with the vehicle and watch everyone coming and going.

After Zach had left, she rummaged around in her bag and retrieved her pistol. She couldn't help feeling that going to Zach's apartment was walking into a trap. She speculated that the trip was the likely reason that the mission was only partially successful. Maybe if she cancelled the trip, the notification would change. However, ultimately, Zach would need to resume his life and he would need things from his place. Finding a new place to live really wouldn't solve his problems, so he would eventually need to return anyway.

Before long, Zach came back to the car with a shopping cart filled with plastic bags. After transferring everything into the trunk, they were under way again.

Glancing over at Zach, Willow asked, "Are you ready to go see how bad it is at your place?" She realized that it would be difficult for anyone as invested in his research as Zach was, to potentially see all his hard work destroyed.

Zach replied, "Yeah. At this point, I'm not sure which is worse, seeing everything wrecked or imagining how bad it is.

At least this way, I'll know."

Willow reached out a hand to offer him a little comfort and her fingers intertwined with Zach's. It felt so right having his solid warm fingers interlaced with hers that she kept them there as they made the four-hour trip to Arlington. When they were close to the city, he gave her occasional instructions that directed her to his apartment.

Zach was worried about the wisdom of returning home, after Willow had pointed out the potential dangers. He knew that he shouldn't encourage the contact, but it was comforting to feel the solid warmth of her fingers interlaced with his.

When they were close, he announced, "This is the street, on the right," followed by, "The brick building in the middle of the block on the left. The parking is around back."

Willow disengaged her fingers and pulled her gun from the pocket in the door alongside her and laid it in her lap as she followed his directions.

As she backed into a space with a straight shot at the entrance/exit, she scanned the lot nervously. She didn't like that they were essentially boxed in with the layout. "Do you recognize all the vehicles?" she asked.

Zach looked around and realized that he didn't know his neighbors well enough to know what they drove. He did see his car it the spot where he had left it. Sheepishly he admitted, "Um, I honestly don't know. I guess so. I get a little preoccupied with my work and haven't really paid much attention, unfortunately."

Willow tried to hide her disappointment. It wasn't fair to expect Zach to be looking for an assassin. With a little shrug, she looked at her watch and directed, "Give me your keys."

Zach handed his apartment key over and said, "There is

a proximity badge on the ring to get in the main door."

Willow looked at the plastic square and key he had handed her and nodded as she said, "Well, let's get going then. Remember, thirty minutes. Once we get inside and I clear the rooms, tell me what I can do to help to make the most out of the time."

Zach heard the phrase 'clear the rooms' and realized that someone could be waiting inside for them. That possibility hadn't occurred to him before now and he again questioned his decision to come. He had no idea if any of his specimens would be salvageable. Was he being foolish to try?

Willow was out of the car and had popped the trunk. Grabbing a couple light plastic bags in one hand, she held her pistol in the other as she scanned the parking lot. Seeing no movement, she motioned for Zach to join her at the back of the car. The trunk offered some protection and she kept scanning her surroundings while he grabbed the rest of the bags. Once the trunk was closed, they were committed.

When the soft thud came, she ordered, "Let's go. Now. Stay next to me and move as quick as you can," as she headed for the back entrance in a light jog.

Zach had bags in each hand, and it wasn't easy to keep up, but he managed. His eyes darted around, looking for a gunman to pop out of the bushes as they neared the building, but no one appeared.

As the door opened, Willow wondered how the intruder had gotten by the decent security measure. As the door closed behind them and they stepped into the hall, Willow held up her arm carrying the bags, blocking Zach's progress as she looked for potential threats. Fortunately, the hall was empty. There was an elevator to one side and Zach stepped in that direction and Willow said, "No. We'll take the stairs," as she nodded to the door opposite the elevator.

Opening the door, she checked around before climbing the stairs as her eyes stayed trained on the flight above them. She hated to scare a resident if they came across one with her exposed gun, but she wasn't willing to risk being caught off guard. "What floor?" she asked as they climbed.

"Third," Zach replied as he stayed close behind Willow. As they passed the door to the second floor, his eyes darted from the stairs above them back toward the way they had come, watching to alert Willow if anyone entered the stairwell behind them.

They arrived at the door to the third floor and Willow opened it a crack as she pressed Zach against the wall with her arm, bumping him in the chest with the bags she carried. Easing her head through, she checked up and down the hall which was thankfully empty as well. It was the middle of the day, after all, and many of the residents were probably still at work. "Right or left?" she asked.

"Left, 317," Zach supplied.

Committing to travelling the last few steps, Willow hugged one side of the hall and Zach followed suit until they arrived at his apartment. There was an X made of crime scene tape attached to the frame and a police seal taped to the door. Willow ignored both and fit the key into the lock, turning the knob to open it. Setting down the bags, she pulled the police tape down and shouldered the door open.

Seeing nothing in the entryway, she motioned Zach in and held a finger up to her lips, pantomiming for him to be quiet. With the door closed behind them, she motioned for Zach to stay put. Then she soundlessly glided off to the right. After checking every room for a lurking intruder and finding no one, she returned to Zach and repeated the process to the left side of the apartment.

After determining that they were alone, she called out,

"Okay, all clear." She checked her watch and called out, "You have twenty minutes left. Tell me what you want me to do."

She had taken in the extent of the damage to Zach's apartment during her sweep and knew that he was going to be upset when he saw it. All the rooms in the apartment had been thoroughly tossed. Zach headed directly to his office which was in the spare bedroom. He had set up half a dozen large aquariums in that room and they had been shattered. All the contents had been drained onto the carpet beneath them. It was obvious that the person had been looking for something. Zach's desktop computer, also in the spare room, had been smashed and the hard drive had been ripped out.

Setting his bags down, Zach pushed aside the disappointment at seeing his years of work ruined as well as the anger at the person who had done so much damage and called out, "Go to the kitchen. Left hand cupboard above the stove. There is an oatmeal container there. Inside there's a sandwich bag with thumb drives on a keyring. Grab them. They are the backups to all my research files. Hopefully whoever did this didn't find them."

As he spoke, Zach rummaged around in the plastic bags he had set on the floor. Straightening, he held two of the glass jars he had purchased. He squirted some brine concentrate from a bottle on a nearby shelf into them. Thankfully, it hadn't leaked even though it had been knocked over in the chaos. Rushing into the bathroom, he ran some water from the tap into each of the jars. Returning to the spare room, he heard Willow yell, "Found them!"

He gave her new instructions, "Open up the drawer under the stove. Inside is a fireproof safe with all my important papers and some cash."

"Clever," Willow called back. Doing as he commanded, she lifted the heavy box out. The intruder hadn't been thorough enough in their search to find either of Zach's hiding spots. Carrying the safe to the entryway she called out, "Where's the key?"

Zach was checking the saline content of each jar with a dipstick. The mixture was close enough for now. He rummaged around his desk drawer and found scissors. Dropping down to his knees, he began scraping algae sludge from the carpet, careful not to cut himself on the pieces of glass scattered around. He replied, "There is a little nail on the backside of the picture hanging over the bed. Right hand side. The key is hooked on it."

Willow followed Zach's instructions and grabbed the key. She was pleased that his hiding spots had been unusual enough that whoever had been here had missed everything vital. "Do you need anything else?" she asked.

Zach thought for a second before he replied, "In the closet, there is a backpack that the contents of the safe should fit in. It would be easier to carry. Oh, and I have some journals under the bathroom sink, behind the toilet paper. I don't use them much anymore but some of my early stuff is in there."

Willow grabbed the items and opened the safe with the key, scooping the contents into the backpack and zipping it closed. She checked her watch. Ten minutes left. She returned to Zach's office and found him cutting pieces of pile from the carpet and putting it into a mason jar of water. There were several sealed jars sitting on the floor.

Zach saw Willow walk in and instructed her. "I have a cooler bag in there," he indicated the mostly empty bags on the floor with his head, "Can you open it up and start packing these jars inside? Maybe grab a couple t-shirts to pack between them?"

Willow quickly did as he directed, and urged, "We need to be on our way out in five more minutes."

Zach screwed the last lid on the jar and handed it to her. Stepping carefully around the glass, he scribbled on a series of post-it notes at the desk. Affixing one to the top of each jar, he lowered the cover flap and zipped it closed. "All set," he pronounced.

Resisting the urge to try to take more things with him, Zach tuned out the shattered glass and all it represented. He focused on the picnic bag full of jars he slung over his shoulder. The carpet had still been damp, and he was hopeful that the specimens he had collected would still be viable. Maybe his years of work were not completely lost.

Willow saw the bleak look in Zach's eye and imagined how hard it was to see his efforts destroyed so savagely. She reached out a hand and interlaced her fingers with his. Gently she urged him, "We need to leave now. I'm sorry."

Zach braced his shoulders. Willow's warm fingers in his were comforting. With a sigh, he said, "I'm ready."

Willow led the way back to the hall where she shrugged into the backpack. Peeking into the hall, she saw no one and motioned for him to follow her. They repeated the process as they retraced their way down the stairs and back to the parking lot entrance.

It had been a stroke of bad luck when Bruno Wilson had gotten kicked off the *Learn of the Sea.* He and his partner had worked out the perfect way to kill Professor Tyler while making it look like a diving accident. His partner had done her best to follow through with the plan, but she had failed.

Improvising several more times, she had still not been able to complete the task so that they could get their payout. She had been communicating with him via sat phone and he knew that his target had flown back stateside. That technology had turned out to be a good investment when they had been separated.

It hadn't been a complete waste of Bruno's time to be stuck on the mainland. He had come up with the idea of wrecking the professor's research in his apartment. He next planned to get into the man's office at the university and take whatever he could find there before setting it on fire. It had been disappointing that, despite having plenty of time to search Zach's place, he hadn't been able to find anything other than the desktop hard drive. Hopefully, everything they wanted would be there when he turned it over to the company paying them.

Bruno thought it likely that the professor would return to his apartment. So, he was headed there now to stake it out. Maybe, like before, he could slip inside with a delivery person. It would be easier to wait inside the apartment and shoot the man when he came home.

Pulling into the parking lot, Bruno found an empty space and parked so that he could see the entrance door. He then pulled out his pistol and settled in to wait. When his target arrived, he would shoot him and drive away. If a delivery arrived before the professor, Bruno would try his plan to wait inside.

A few minutes later, he was surprised to see Tyler exiting the building carrying a soft-sided cooler strapped over one shoulder. There was a tall blonde woman with him, and she was in the way of getting off a clean shot. They were sprinting quickly across the open area of the parking lot and he would soon have no shot to take. Deciding he couldn't worry about the woman, Bruno quickly pointed the gun and squeezed off several rounds.

Willow noticed a different car backed into a parking space as she pressed the remote to unlock their car. It hadn't been there when they had arrived. Hurrying Zach along, they were only a few steps from her car when a flash of sunlight on metal caught her eye. "Get down!" she urged Zach as she crouched lower and trained her gun on the new vehicle where she could see a pistol barrel sticking out of the driver's window.

Firing a shot of her own, her bullet made a mark where it impacted the car, just below the side mirror. Adjusting her aim, she squeezed off another shot and saw the front passenger window shatter. The shooter wasn't hanging around any longer. With a rev of the engine and squealing tires, the car sped away. The driver took one more shot in their general direction, but Willow ducked, using the rental car as a shield. Hearing the sound of shattering glass, she turned to look over her shoulder and saw that the shot had starred a windshield several cars away.

Turning back to Zach, she saw that he had opened the rear passenger door and climbed inside, keeping low in the back seat as he stowed his precious specimens on the floor. Zach's heart was pounding in his ears. After the shooting, the silence seemed eerie. He heard the driver's door open and poked his head up to see Willow lowering herself into the seat behind the wheel.

Locking her gaze with Zach's in the rearview mirror, Willow said, "You should probably stay back there and keep your head down. The shooter took off but may follow us and try again."

Zach swallowed nervously and nodded. He felt like he was trapped in some sci-fi movie where everyone was trying to kill him. He felt like he would never be safe again. He sank back down on the back seat and stared up at the ceiling as he felt Willow pull out of the parking space and drive away. He was a man who was used to doing things for himself and using his brain to solve his problems. It was frustrating that he was having to rely on someone else to stay alive. Although, if he was forced to rely on another person, Willow was proving herself very capable in her role of protector.

He felt the car make several more turns and stops. He realized they would soon be on the freeway. "Any sign that we are being followed?" he asked.

"Yeah. Pretty sure he's back there," was her terse reply.

Willow was worried that once they were on the freeway and travelling at a faster speed, their shooter would just have to nudge their bumper from behind and their light economy car would be sent spinning. She wasn't hopeful that the vehicle would have the engine power to outrun the one following them either. She had an idea but, until she saw the freeway traffic, she didn't know if it would work. If she elected to stay on the surface streets, the shooter likely would eventually grow impatient and take more shots. Such a thing could cause unpredictable collateral damage.

Checking the rearview mirror, she cautioned, "Hang on," as she jerked the steering wheel harshly to the right as she punched the gas pedal, turning them onto an on-ramp.

The traffic wasn't too heavy, although there were several cars nearby as she merged in with them. Looking back, she saw the dark car following them had made the maneuver as well.

The truck right behind them changed lanes and exited the freeway, leaving the back of Willow's car exposed. She watched in the mirrors as the vehicle gained on them.

With her eyes darting to the side and further up the freeway, she saw what she needed to do. Pressing the accelerator to the floor, the engine hesitated for a moment before the car jumped forward. As soon as they were clear of the vehicle alongside them, she cut the wheel hard to the left and shot across the lane and continued their sharp angle to catch the exit ramp on the far side of the freeway. As the tires met that pavement, she mashed on the brakes while fighting to maintain control as the exit ramp curved away sharply. The car fishtialed a bit but she managed to keep it on the road. Thankfully, there were not many cars stopped at the light at the end of the ramp and she was able to bring the car to a halt.

As she watched the ramp behind them in the mirror, she asked, "Doing okay back there?"

Zach's big frame hadn't fit well in the back seat and he was feeling a little tossed around, but he replied gamely, "All good here."

The light turned green and Willow drove off on the surface street. Another car came down the ramp, but it wasn't the one she had been worried about. Breathing a sigh of relief, she looked around for a place they could park for a few minutes. She needed help finding a secure location for them to hide out for a bit while she tried to come up with a new plan.

Spotting a self-serve car wash, Willow turned in and drove down to an empty stall on the far end of the complex and pulled in. Placing the car in park and shutting off the engine, she turned to Zach and said, "Okay, you can sit up now," as she pulled out her communicator.

Looking at the screen she saw that the percentage was back to fifteen and she frowned. Since she had just saved Zach yet again, it made no sense that the likelihood of her mission succeeding had gotten worse. They were no better off now than they had been when they were on the boat.

CHAPTER FIFTEEN

Willow considered this change as she sent off a message to Commander Keene requesting a safe location to lay low for a few days. Preferably someplace with some sunshine so that Zach's algae could get an opportunity to grow. Everything that was happening now was a deviation from the original timeline and she had no clues that would offer an explanation for their continued failure. She had thought she was doing a decent job keeping Zach safe. So, why wasn't it making a difference?

As she pressed send, she had an idea. "Zach, why don't you power up your phone and see if you have any messages."

Zach had seen her communicator's screen over her shoulder and felt a stab of disappointment. After everything they had been through just now, how could it all have been for nothing? He was surprised by her suggestion and asked, "Are you sure I should? What if whoever is after me uses the signal to locate us?"

Willow voiced her suspicions. "I don't think that we are dealing with professional killers here. If we were, they wouldn't have missed while we were at sea and they definitely wouldn't have missed at your place. If I were doing the job, I would have set a bomb to go off in the apartment."

Zach shuddered inwardly as he considered what she had revealed with that comment. He was definitely glad Willow was on his side.

She continued, "Also, we were able to get away from the driver just now. I'm thinking that they probably lack the computer hacking skills to locate you, especially if you are on and off quickly. I need to figure out what has happened because my communicator is telling me that you still don't succeed in bringing your research to reality. Maybe something on your phone will give us a clue about what we need to change or fix."

The idea seemed logical to Zach and, if Willow thought it was safe, he was eager to see how the efforts to secure his replacement were going and if the police had found any leads on who had broken into his place. He turned on his phone and, after about a minute, started scrolling through his emails. He opened one from the University with bold capital letters in the subject line that stated, "IMMEDIATE ACTION REQUIRED".

As Zach started reading, a wave of anger washed over him. Unable to keep his frustration to himself, he burst out, "This is just SO wrong! I didn't do anything to deserve this accusation!"

Willow asked as a wave of apprehension washed over her, "What accusation?"

Zach quickly finished the email before he paraphrased, "Apparently, one of the students aboard ship has accused me of inappropriately suggesting sexual favors would be a way to secure a 4.0 grade in the class."

Unable to resist responding to the baseless claim, he began typing a response vehemently denying the student's allegation.

Willow interrupted him, "Who was the student?"

Zach looked up and stopped typing. "Her name is Mindy. I was so preoccupied with my experiment I could just vaguely describe her to you. I certainly never spent any time alone with her. I was spending all my free time with you." With that reminder, he asked, "Would you mind if I use our shipboard time together as my alibi?"

Willow replied, "Yes, of course." Her mind was processing this latest development. It would explain why Zach's research never was developed. If he lost his position and funding through the University, Zach would be discredited in scientific circles. It actually was a smart move. Why kill Zach if he could be professionally ruined. Whoever was behind these attacks would only have to pay off another female student Zach had once taught. When a second student came forward, despite the lack of any real evidence, the University would fire Zach. Willow was convinced that this was the reason that her success meter was back to such a low percentage. Character assassination was harder to defend against than an actual attempt on Zach's life.

Willow's communicator chimed a response and she looked at the coordinates listed along with an overlying map. They would have to drive several hours to reach the place indicated and it looked remote. She wasn't sure what they would find when they got there so she needed to make a couple stops to prepare.

"I have a place for us to go for a few days," she announced.

"Finish sending your message as I drive. Tell them that you're innocent and that you were having an affair with me. I'll vouch for your conduct aboard the ship. Mindy was the student parading around in her bikini that first day. She's probably miffed that you didn't actually come on to her.

Maybe mention some of that tactfully in your reply," Willow suggested as she pulled out of the car wash and began looking for a store that would have what she needed.

She continued, "We need to look at this in a positive manner. By making the accusation, she has identified herself as one of the people after you on the ship. Although she couldn't be the person who just shot at us, at least we finally have a name and face for one of your attackers."

She could hear Zach typing away for a few minutes before he leaned back with a sigh and powered off the phone. "Well, that's done." He was still fuming over the accusation. "I can't believe the dean would be talking about firing me because of one baseless accusation. I asked him to get in touch with Captain Harvey and ask if there was any inappropriate behavior he noticed."

Willow said, "That was a good idea." Softly she added, trying to prepare Zach for what she worried about, "You shouldn't be surprised when another female student comes forward. The company behind this could pay off several more students from your past and have them make with claims of their own."

Shock washed over Zach. Removing his glasses, he buried his face in his hands. With despair in his muffled voice, he asked, "How can all this be happening to me? I've worked so hard to get where I'm at. And, I've always been so careful about working with female students and assistants. What am I going to do?"

"I'm not sure yet," Willow replied. "Let's try to figure everything out over the next couple days." Wanting to offer him some hope, she added, "I'm sure that we will think of something. I know that it must be difficult but try not to get too discouraged yet."

Seeing a store that might have all the supplies she

needed, Willow turned off the street and found a parking spot. Turning to Zach she said, "I'm not really comfortable with splitting up. But, just in case these people are better than I think, I don't want your face on any of the store cameras. I'll be gone for a little bit. Are you comfortable shooting my gun if you need to?"

Zach shook his head.

Willow went on, "Do you mind if I use some of the cash I saw when I emptied your safe?"

He nodded. So much had happened in such a short amount of time that his mind was spinning as Zach struggled with what to focus on first. Realizing that he hadn't gotten past that one email, he asked, "Do you think it would be safe for me to power up my phone again? There may be more messages I need to deal with."

Willow could see that Zach was trying to hold himself together. She speculated that it wouldn't be likely that someone would be able to hack the phone or police systems to triangulate his phone's position and arrive at their location before she would be back with their supplies. "Sure. Go ahead," she said as she left the car. She stopped to pull a baseball cap from her duffle in the trunk and stuffed her long blonde hair up underneath it. It wasn't the best disguise, but maybe the shooter hadn't gotten a good look at her.

Hurrying inside the store, she grabbed a cart and went to the camping section. In such a rural location, Willow thought it was possible that they would need outdoor gear for where they were going. She also chose a cooler that could be packed with ice to store any perishable food items. Then she went to the grocery section. As she loaded a case of bottled water into the cart, she knew that Zach would cringe at the single use plastics, but she wanted to make sure that they had drinking water.

Her cart was heaped full when she was done shopping and she chafed as she had to wait in line for the cashier. She felt the minutes passing and worried about her estimate that they would be gone before anyone would be able to track Zach's phone. What if she had made a terrible mistake letting him use it? What if, even now, he was being gunned down in the parking lot?

Zach was reading an email from the detective who had been assigned to his apartment break-in. As he had anticipated, the man said that they didn't have any leads. Zach sent off a message informing the detective that he had time-sensitive material in the apartment that he had needed to recover so he had broken the police seal. He also decided to report the attempted shooting, since it was likely that the police had already been called about the damage from the bullets. Zach told the detective that he didn't know who was behind it, which was true. But he didn't share their suspicions as to why someone had tried to kill him. He ended the message by saying that he was going into hiding for a while because he feared for his life.

After that, Zach sent off another email to his dean. In it he raised the concern that the student was disgruntled after having her advances rebuffed. He thought about the time he had spent with Willow. He didn't think that he could classify what was between them as a relationship, but he found himself wishing that it was. She had been clear from the beginning that she was in this time for the purpose of protecting him. There was no mention of how long she might be here, but he knew it was implied that she would be leaving when her work was finished.

Zach was fighting with the attraction that he felt for her. She was a combination of all the things he found attractive in a woman. She was smart, confident, and beautiful. Normally, he was so absorbed in his work that he didn't notice women in a sexual way. However, Willow had had his attention from their first interaction. He found himself indulging physically in a way he seldom had since his college days. Why was it that the most interesting woman he had met in a long time was only temporarily passing through his life?

Still, Zach decided to elaborate on his feelings for Willow in the email to his dean. He talked about thinking that he had found the one woman for him and realized that it was the truth. He also reminded his boss that he was highly devoted to his research with algae and would never dream of doing anything that would jeopardize what he viewed as his life's work. After pressing send, he scrolled through his other messages.

There was a commotion alongside the car as someone opened the door of the vehicle next to him. Startled, Zach realized that he should be more aware of what was going on around him. Deciding that he had spent enough time on his phone, he powered it down and slouched down in the seat after angling himself so that he could watch the parking lot behind the car. There were people and vehicles coming and going as the store was very busy. Still, he thought that one car had circled the lot several times. Maybe he was being paranoid. Checking his watch, he realized that Willow had been gone almost an hour. Surely, she would be returning soon.

Finally, he heaved a mental sigh of relief when he saw Willow returning. She was pushing a cart heaped full of bags.

She opened the trunk and unloaded what she could inside. The rest of her purchases would have to fit in the car.

Opening the back door, Willow was relieved to see Zach appeared unharmed. She smiled broadly and said, "Did you miss me?"

Zach was relieved she was back and said with a broad grin of his own, "You bet I did. I was starting to think that every circling car was looking for me."

Willow stilled, a bag in her hand as she looked around quickly. Seeing no eminent threat, she hastily stowed the rest of the gear as she asked, "What did the car look like?"

Zach was feeling foolish for his earlier suspicions and was surprised that Willow was taking him so seriously. "Um, a dark blue sedan, I think," he replied.

With the cart now empty, Willow commanded, "Stay down out of sight," as she closed the door. After placing the cart in a nearby corral, she climbed in behind the wheel. The car that had followed them on the freeway had been a dark blue sedan. Pulling out of the parking spot, she drove at a leisurely pace, not trying to draw attention to them. There was no evidence of a dark sedan following them as they pulled out into the street. She was thankful that she had insisted on renting a grey car in a popular model. Since there were other ones like it in the lot, it made them harder to find.

Willow kept watching in her mirrors as they put several miles between them and the store. Seeing no evidence of being followed, she pulled into a gas station to fill up and get their groceries packed into the cooler. With the added supplies, the back seat was quite cramped for Zach and she asked, "Doing okay back there? Think you can wait for another couple miles? I don't want the cameras here to pick you up if you move to the front seat now. Even if our assassin doesn't have access to facial recognition software, the police are probably looking for you after the shooting at your apartment."

Zach worried now about the message he had sent them. "Um, while I was waiting at the store, I replied to the detective and told him that I was going into hiding. Maybe I shouldn't have done that. I admitted that I had broken the police seal on my door." Belatedly, he realized his mistake. "That probably was a crime itself, wasn't it?"

Willow tried to hide the fact that she was disappointed by his admission. "Well, let's give it a few days and see how things develop." She hoped that the detective would see it as a petty crime and not try to find Zach. It was one thing to try eluding people she was more and more convinced were amateurs. Trying to hide from the police was another matter altogether.

CHAPTER SIXTEEN

Willow drove following the directions provided by her communicator. When they were well outside the city, on a stretch of road surrounded by farmland, she pulled over and Zach moved to the front passenger seat. It felt nice to get out and stretch his legs.

After she was comfortable that they weren't being followed, Willow relaxed a little and they talked about a variety of things, including Zach's hopes that he had been able to salvage some of the other strains of algae he had been cultivating.

The flat farmland gave way to rolling fields of pastures and wooded hills. In the distance, they could see the shadowy mountains drawing closer. Soon, they were climbing steeper grades and Willow slowed to carefully navigate the turns in the road. As the sun was setting, they passed through a small, sleepy village. Soon after that, they were instructed to turn off the paved road onto a dirt track that took them deeper into the woods. Willow hoped that the road didn't get any rougher. The economy car wasn't four-wheel drive and she doubted the suspension would hold up if it got too much more bumpy.

Her headlights were cutting through the gloom under the canopy of trees as she slowly worked her way along. Then, the trees opened up and their headlights illuminated what was likely a hunting cabin. It was small but seemed to be in good repair.

Coming to a stop, she said, "Well, this must be the place."

There were no lights on in the structure and none came on with their arrival. However, that didn't mean that the place was unoccupied. She doubted that Commander Keene would send her to a place that was already inhabited, but several hundred years separated them and it would be impossible for the AIs to know if vagrants had taken up residence.

Picking up her gun, she doused the headlights before she opened the car door as she said to Zach, "Stay here. I'm going to go check the place out."

She rummaged around in the back of the car and found a flashlight which she tested before closing the trunk again. Then, giving her eyes a moment to adjust to the darkness, Willow worked her way to the side of the cabin rather than walking up to the front door. Easing toward the small window with her back against the log siding, she took a look inside. Seeing nothing, she risked shining the flashlight in through to glass.

The cabin seemed to be one large room and there was no evidence that it had been occupied recently. She moved to the porch and up the steps. In the glow of the flashlight, she could see a foreclosure notice taped to the inside of the front door. Trying the knob, Willow found it locked. Slipping her gun into her jeans at the small of her back, she pulled out her lock picks. With a few deft twists of her wrists, the door swung in with only a small squeak.

Willow again drew her pistol and inspected the cabin. As she had thought, it was just one room with a fireplace on one end and a loft above the kitchen area. There was a small curtained bathroom next to the kitchen. After making sure that no one else was around, she returned to the door and tried the light switch next to it. Nothing happened. Either the power had been turned off or there was a generator that needed attention.

Willow sighed inwardly. It had been a very long, intense day and the adrenaline that had been driving her seemed to fade away, leaving her mentally and physically exhausted. There was still a lot of unpacking they needed to do, and she couldn't remember the last time she had eaten. Digging deep to keep moving, she headed back to the car and Zach.

Together, they hauled in all of their things. The first priority for them was getting warm. The mountain air was cool and rapidly turning to cold. "Do you know how to make a fire?" she asked.

Zach shook his head, "No, my parents always sent me to science camp. While you might think that making fire would be a good experiment, we had Bunsen burners to roast marshmallows over."

Willow had brought matches and fire starter, so she wasn't worried about that part. Looking around, she saw that the wood box next to the fireplace was empty. "Why don't you take the flashlight and see if there is any firewood or dead sticks around that we can burn," she suggested.

"Sure thing," Zach replied.

After he was gone, Willow crouched down in front of the fireplace. It would do no good to start a fire if there was no place for the smoke to go. She hoped that an animal hadn't nested in the chimney, blocking it up. She hadn't looked at the date on the foreclosure notice, but the paper was curled on the edges and faded. The place had a layer of dust on everything, so Willow suspected that it had been vacant for some time.

She found the damper knob and wiggled it a few times. Debris came raining down. After another couple turns, the flue seemed free. She knelt again and looked up. While it was dark outside, she thought she glimpsed some stars. Rising, she turned to unpacking some food while she waited for Zach to return.

A few minutes later, he was back with an armful of wood. "There is a little bit of old firewood stacked against the back of the cabin," he reported. "I'll grab another load which should get us through the night."

"If you can, grab me some smaller sticks too," she requested.

Opening a granola bar, she knew she should probably wait for Zach, but she was too hungry. The snack would tide her over until the fire was lit and they were ready for a real meal.

When Zach returned, the wood box was full, and Willow went to work on the fire. She started with a stack of small sticks. If the chimney wasn't working, they would know before the whole cabin filled with smoke.

She said, "See if you can open one of the windows just a crack." Willow figured that the move might improve the draw of the chimney as she blew gently on her burgeoning fire. The flames took off and smoke didn't seem to be rolling back into the cabin. Cautiously optimistic, she put a larger piece of wood into the flames and stood. Zach was nearby, watching her, and he looked as tired as she felt.

"Why don't we lay out the sleeping bags and get some

rest," she suggested. There would be time in the light of the next day to finish unpacking. "There are some granola bars as well as bread and lunchmeat if you want to make a sandwich," she said as she began unrolling the foam pads that would provide a little cushion under the sleeping bags.

Zach was munching on one of the bars as she finished laying one pad in front of the fireplace and turned to open the other one. Their intimacy sharing his bunk on the boat seemed like such a long time ago. He longed to gather her close as they slept. He spoke up, "You know, if you zipped those sleeping bags together, we could keep each other warm if the fire went out overnight."

Willow's eyes shot to his. The thought of leisurely exploring the hard planes of his body while lying next to the fire warred with her fatigue. "It does sound like a practical solution," she agreed. "But, I'm so tired right now all I can think about is sleep."

Zach considered everything she had been doing on his behalf throughout the day and saw the fatigue in her eyes. Stepping away from the food, he came over and drew her into his arms. "I'm sorry that I haven't really thanked you for saving me so many times today. I seem to be making a daily habit out of needing you to rescue me. I'm normally a pretty self-sufficient guy. And, thank you for helping me get everything from my place. You were right about it being a trap and maybe it wasn't worth the risk, but I'm glad I was able to save some of my other algae."

Willow thought about what it must be like for Zach. He was smart but totally unprepared for fending off the constant attacks that were coming their way. She was uncomfortable with his praise, though. She felt like she was failing him because nothing she did seemed to improve his situation. Trying to lighten the moment a bit she replied, "Well, it's a good thing you aren't an ass. It's easy to protect you because I like you. Now, come on. We are both nearly sleeping on our feet. Let's get some rest. We still have a lot to do in the morning."

They settled into the sleeping bag in front of the fire. As they were lying side by side but not touching, Willow soon heard the soft breaths that told her Zach was asleep. As she lay on her side mesmerized by the dancing flames licking the block of wood, she considered her words to Zach. She had done other protection jobs where her charge had been difficult and resisted her efforts to keep them safe. Sometimes, on other protection assignments, she had found herself wishing that she could do the honors to dispatch her charge herself. However, as frustrating as those situations had been, she thought that this mission was more complicated because she genuinely cared about what happened to Zach. It had been drilled into her during her TEP training that she should never become involved with her assignments. She was starting to worry that her attraction to Zach was clouding her judgment.

The next morning came all too quickly. The wooden floor wasn't the best mattress, despite the foam padding. Willow had awakened first, to find Zach spooning her in their snug cocoon. She extricated herself as quickly as she could, despite the stiff muscles that had developed overnight. She used the excuse of tending the fire to keep her back to Zach as she spoke, "Better get moving. I figure that you'll want to inspect your samples to make sure that they are in good shape."

The morning passed quickly as they cooked breakfast and hunted for more firewood. In the afternoon, Zach

inspected the containers that held his specimens and pronounced everything was satisfactory. Willow had decided to
try to find out more about Mindy, now that they knew she was
involved. Surprisingly, there was a decent wi-fi signal at the
cabin, so she hacked into the woman's social media accounts.
She found a series of pictures of Mindy with various hair
colors and styles. Interestingly, Willow recognized the man
in many of the pictures with her. He was the crew member she
had gotten kicked off the ship. Willow realized that with the
two of them working together, it was no wonder an unsus-
pecting Zach had been so easily killed in the original timeline.

With her fingers flying over the keyboard, Willow established an untraceable link and forwarded the pics to Zach's
dean and the police along with the suggestion that they check
into the couple's bank activity. She hoped that it would be
enough for the dean to believe Zach.

As it grew dark, they ate their evening meal compan-
ionably. Willow asked about the samples and explained
what she had discovered. Zach was feeling hopeful at the new
information.

When they had cleaned up after dinner, Willow was
starting to get nervous. She was so aware of Zach and kept repeating to herself all the reasons that she shouldn't give in to
her attraction for him again.

Zach could sense that Willow was uncomfortable.
Trying to find some neutral ground, he asked, "In all the things
you bought, you didn't happen to include a deck of cards or a
book, did you?"

Willow shook her head ruefully, "No, unfortunately. I
should have thought of something like that."

Zach paced around the tiny room as his mind looked
for a safe topic of conversation. "Well, I suppose we could play
twenty questions," he began. He hadn't thought of the child-

hood game in years.

Willow didn't want to play games though she appreciated that Zach was trying to fill their time. She went back to her computer and said, "I'm going to hack into your email account to see if there is anything new from the University or the police."

Zach perked up, "That's a great idea. Maybe the dean will have decided Mindy's accusation doesn't have merit. He watched as Willow checked her communicator and saw that it still registered fifteen percent. Disappointment caused his shoulders to slump. When would this nightmare ever end? He leaned over Willow's shoulder and watched as she worked on her computer. The scent of her hair tickled his nose and increased his awareness of her. Despite his best intentions, he felt his dick stir.

Willow tried to focus on the words on the screen as she felt Zach's warm chest brush her shoulder occasionally. There was a message from the dean in which Zach was being summoned to face the accusation and provide an accounting of his research to date.

Zach hung his head, "That sounds to me like the university is going to hand my project over to another researcher."

Willow twisted to face him, "How can they do that? You developed the algae. They can't give it to someone else to take credit for, can they?"

Zach saw her angry expression and smiled ruefully, "My work while in their employ is technically their intellectual property. They can take me off the project if they want to."

Willow thought about how the future hadn't been changed and said, "But that move won't make the project happen."

"Perhaps the next researcher will be more easily bought off by the company behind all this," he suggested.

Willow was frustrated. She closed the laptop and began pacing the room. "There must be something we can do to change the dean's mind."

After a few more minutes of thinking and getting nowhere, she mentally threw in the towel. "We need to turn in. Maybe after a good night's sleep, something will come to us." Looking at the sleeping bag laid out before the fire, Willow figured that she wasn't likely to get much rest with her heightened awareness of Zach.

By silent agreement, they kept their backs to each other as they changed. Zach thought that it was going to be a long, uncomfortable night. Throwing another chunk of wood into the fire while Zach settled into the bag, Willow turned back to see the desire in his eyes.

Zach had been trying to keep his mind off Willow's long bare legs, but when her breasts were backlit by the fire, he was mesmerized. He watched as they swayed under the thin cotton as she moved to tend the fire and his cock was instantly hard.

Having put off joining Zach as long as she could, Willow knelt down and slid in. When she rolled to her side with her back towards him, Zach let out a sigh and said, "Willow, I don't know if you are angry at me for something? I feel like we had a good thing on the boat. Are you regretting what we did?"

She rolled over towards him, her face in shadows as she replied, "I'm not normally so quick to let down my guard, Zach. You've sort of thrown me off kilter and I don't know what to do about it. I realize that I'm probably confusing you by being all hot and cold and I'm sorry for that. I keep trying to remind myself that I should focus on my mission. What if my distraction results in you being harmed?"

Zach appreciated her single-mindedness, but it rankled a bit that she didn't think he could take care of himself. Shifting to his side so that his face was only inches from hers, he whispered, "We are in the middle of nowhere. I'm willing to take my chances." He thought her words described his feelings as well. "The previous times we were together, everything was so intense. I really want to take the time to savor being with you." Unable to resist her mouth any longer, he leaned over gently pressed his lips to hers.

At the contact, Willow couldn't resist any longer. She wrapped her arms around his shoulders, closed her eyes, and snuggled in closer. Zach brought his arm around her and drew her hips up against his pelvis. She could feel a bulge growing against her stomach.

He lifted his lips and shifted to run his tongue around the whorls of her ear before drawing the lobe gently between his teeth. Then he murmured into her ear and his words tickled as he spoke, "This is way more interesting than twenty questions."

Willow was feeling the tickle of his mouth all the way to her core. At his words, she couldn't suppress the giggle that escaped. She grinned as she said, "I agree. I'm done fighting with myself, at lease for now. This sounds to me like the perfect way to spend a night alone in the woods."

Zach's head lowered to close the scant distance between them again, and excitement pulsed through her. His kiss was soft and exploring without being aggressive. He seemed content to let the attraction build slowly. She was delighting in the play of his lips and the way his tongue stoked the pleasure in her as it dove in and out.

At some point, they separated enough for her t-shirt to come off. Her pale skin took on an amber glow in the firelight. The cool air on her exposed nipples caused them to tighten under his gaze. As the light danced across her upper chest, Zach couldn't keep from bending his head to follow its path with his tongue. Her arms wrapped around his shoulders, drawing herself closer. If possible, his cock got even harder, straining at the fabric covering it.

After a few more minutes of languid kissing, he slid his hand down the outside her hip to softly cup her buttocks. At the contact, Willow ran her hands down the smooth muscles of his back. She slid her hands under the waistband of his sleep pants and down to squeeze his butt cheeks. Shifting one hand around so that it was between them, she worked the fabric down over his bulging penis, allowing it to spring free. The hot, silky length of him rubbed against her bare stomach and she was eager to have him inside her. Zach shifted away to kick free of his sleepwear.

He then reached up to cup a breast, its weight filling his palm as he rubbed a calloused thumb over the sensitive tip. Then Zach bent his head again as he closed his warm lips over the other peak. Willow tipped her head back, giving him easier access and released a groan as the pleasure shot from her nipples straight to her core. The gentle pulling of his mouth and the rhythmic abrasion of his thumb felt intense. As her pleasure built, she could feel moisture dampening her panties.

In a hurry, Willow hooked a thumb under the edge of her underwear and drew them down. Zach helped her as she shifted until they were gone. Zach wanted to savor this time together and refused to let her rush him. Leisurely, he drew his palm back up the outside of her thigh and then dipped a finger into her silken folds. She was slick and ready for him, but he held himself back. Instead, he brought his mouth back to her breast, sucking the tight tip in and flicking it with his tongue.

Willow groaned her pleasure as she felt the wave building in her. Then she felt Zach's fingers again between her legs.

He slid a finger into her slickened passage and began circling her clit with his thumb. Frissons of electricity shot through her and she held her breath a moment before letting out a harsh sound that urged him to continue.

He worked his finger in and out in a steady rhythm as he continued to circle her clit and kept working her nipple with his mouth. She tossed her head from side to side, restlessly and her groan had more desperation in its tone. He pushed a second finger inside her and quickened his rhythm. Within moments, with the additional stretch, the wave of pleasure shot through her and she tensed, bucking on his hand as he continued to stroke her throughout her orgasm.

As the pleasure faded and her limbs were lax, he withdrew his fingers and resettled himself between her spread legs. He leaned down with his mouth hovering over hers as he said, "This is even better than playing cards." Then his mouth settled over hers again and he began rebuilding the heat in her. He used his mouth and teeth on her neck and one hand kept kneading her breast and tweaking the sensitized tip.

Willow was shocked at how quickly she was climbing right back to the edge of pleasure. "Definitely better than cards. Now stop playing," she urged him with a breathy voice.

He took her words as encouragement and shifted a little between her legs before sliding smoothly into her to the hilt. Her inner muscles stretched with his rigid fullness. He paused, savoring the warm squeeze of her body but only for a moment as the sensations pushed him to rhythmically withdraw and drive deeper into her.

Impossibly, she felt she was spiraling to higher pleasure than she had experienced mere minutes ago. Willow wrapped her legs around his hips, rocking and meeting him in his rhythm. Zach tried to keep the rhythm slow but felt the wave building at the base of his spine as he ground his teeth and tried to hold on. His breathing was coming in harsh gasps. Their bodies had grown slick with the exertion and pleasure and their torsos were now sliding as they rubbed against each other. He was moving faster and heard her breathing quicken as she panted and moaned, "Oh yes! Zach!"

He gritted his teeth and pumped into her a couple more times until she flew over the edge and her inner muscles clenched rhythmically around him in her release. That was all he needed to follow her over the edge, his balls contracting as he pumped into her. Zach shifted to her side as he collapsed, not wanting her to take his entire weight. The sounds of their harsh breaths and the crackling of the nearby fire were the only sounds in the quiet room.

Now that they were sated, Willow's concerns about the wisdom of indulging in their pleasure returned. Resolutely, she pushed them aside and decided to enjoy feeling surrounded by the silken heat of Zach's naked body. As she drifted off to sleep, she had an idea that would be a way to protect Zach. He saw her satisfied smile moments before sleep claimed him too.

CHAPTER SEVENTEEN

Willow awoke eager to put her plan in motion. She had come to the realization that she cared about what happened to Zach. After the sex they had shared the previous night, she was done trying to deny it. While her idea may be a long shot, at the moment, it was the only solution she could come up with as a way to keep him safe and advance his research. She hadn't wanted to share too much with him so she just said that she had an idea to pursue. That meant they would need to head to Washington so she could make a jump back to her own time. When she packed her bag, she placed a strange-looking wide belt on top of it.

Zach had been perplexed by Willow's suggestion. "Are you going back and leaving me here to deal with everything on my own?" Anger flared within him at the thought. He felt a real connection to her and had thought, especially after last night, that she felt the same. Now, she seemed to be abandoning him. "It feels like I am in more trouble now than I was when I met you. How will I salvage my career?"

Willow pointed out bluntly, "Before you met me, you had no idea what trouble you were in. Remember, you were supposed to have died a few days ago. I need you to trust me a little bit longer. I think that I may have figured out a way to both keep you safe and allow you to see your research have a real-world impact. However, trying to explain it all to my superior through my communicator would be too difficult. The beauty of time travel is that I can leave you, be in my time for weeks or months if need be, and then return to you seemingly only minutes after I left. You won't even have time to miss me."

Zach was reluctant to leave. They seemed safe in this mountain hideaway. Still, he supposed that they would have to get more supplies eventually, so it wasn't a long-term solution. He felt confused by her plan. But, deciding that he didn't have many alternatives, he reeluctantly agreed to go.

Willow heard the distant sound of a helicopter as they were repacking the car. When she heard it a second time, a little louder now, she recognized that someone was likely flying a grid pattern looking for them. "It's time to leave, Zach," she announced. "I think someone is close to finding us. I don't want to be trapped here since there is only one way out."

Quickly throwing the rest of the gear in, Zach hopped into the passenger seat and fastened his seat belt. As Willow began winding the car through the trees as quickly as she dared, she filled him in. "I heard a helicopter working its way closer. My guess is that it's the police. They would have the ability to track your phone even when it's off. I hesitated to ask before because I figured you might have important information on it, but can you destroy it?"

Zach thought for a moment. Pulling his laptop from his backpack at his feet, he said, "Let me transfer everything to my laptop and then I can." After tethering it, he pressed the keys he needed and completed the download. As he unplugged the cord, he started to roll down the window to toss the phone and she stopped him, "Wait. Don't throw it away. We don't want anyone else getting a hold of it. Crush it with your heel."

Zach did as she instructed, and the screen shattered. He tried to turn it on again and the screen stayed dark. "I think that did it," he informed her.

While she kept checking the skies above them, they traveled most of the day without any further sign that they were being followed. Zach asked Willow about some of the times and places she had visited. As she drove, she told him lots of stories of interesting things that had happened on her missions. She shared some of the famous historical figures she had met. As the rental car covered the miles, Zach found himself envious of the situations she had been in.

2018, Washington Nationals Stadium, District of Columbia, United States

It was well after dark when they drove back into Washington, D.C. Willow made her way to the stadium, unsure if there would be a home game being played that night. However, when they drove around it, the field lights were turned off and it looked deserted. Finding a dark alley not far away, Willow backed the rental in between the dumpsters piled up with garbage.

Willow was a little nervous about this part of her plan. They would be carrying a lot more than she had been when she had jumped into this time. Also, the guards were more alert for people trying to break in as opposed to people suddenly appearing and breaking out. She figured that they might get noticed but, hopefully, not right away.

Moving to the back of the car, Willow slid the pistol

into the small of her back before strapping her time belt around her hips. Then she hoisted her gear bag and Zach's backpack onto one shoulder and picked up one of the two buckets. Zach slung his cooler bag over his shoulder before picking up the other bucket.

"Stay close behind me," she instructed and, without looking back, she headed for the stadium.

They stayed in the shadows of the buildings as they moved along the sidewalk. When the came to one of the metal doors that shuttered an entrance to the stadium, she set down her bucket and whipped out the lock picks. Zach wasn't really surprised when, moments later, she bent to carefully raise it up. Then, looking for any sign that security was aware of them, Willow took care of the lock on the scissor gate before moving it to the side. Motioning Zach through, she shifted her bucket inside and rolled the door back down on its track.

There was no sound of footsteps or glare from flash-lights, so she whispered, "Come on," as she scampered to the stairway across the concourse. Zach found himself climbing stairs and was laboring under his burden a bit as they reached the top. Willow paused only long enough to make sure that security wasn't patrolling in the grandstands before beginning their descent.

When they reached the barricade that separated the stands from the playing field, she set her bucket down and hopped over onto the dirt of the warning track. Zach could see that they were near one of the dugouts. Willow motioned for him to hand her his burdens which he did, grateful for lightening his load, even for a moment. His shoulder muscles were feeling the burn of carrying everything all the way from the car. Once he had passed everything to her, he eased over the low wall himself. "We're almost there," she encouraged as she hurried them to the shadows of the dugout. Her eyes kept darting around, looking for security.

When they stepped down into the shadows, Willow turned to Zach and said, "Stay right here. For you, it will only seem like I have been gone for a few minutes." She didn't know if Commander Bishop would agree with her solution to Zach's problems. But she felt confident that he would send her back and she would be seeing Zach again.

Zach didn't know what to say. What if she didn't come back, despite her promise? How long should he wait here if she didn't?

Willow couldn't resist stretching up on her tiptoes to plant a quick kiss on his lips. Then she dropped his backpack on the bench alongside them before she forced herself to turn her back and sprint away toward the mound. With her elbow, she nudged the first button to activate her belt. She knew that Zach would still be standing next to his containers of algae if she dared to turn back to look. She didn't want to see the hurt she had glimpsed in his eyes. She knew that he didn't really understand what she was doing but she hoped he would trust her a little longer. It surprised her that she was so reluctant to leave him behind.

As her feet hit the dirt of the pitcher's mound, she took a deep breath and elbowed the button to make the time jump. While Zach watched, Willow simply disappeared. He blinked and blinked again. Perhaps on some level, he hadn't been convinced about the validity of her claim to be from the future. However, there was no denying that she had literally vanished into thin air. He no longer doubted time travel was real.

But, in the silence that surrounded him, Zach felt very alone. As he looked down at the samples that represented his life's work, he realized that he could be charged with trespassing if he was discovered here. How would he possibly explain his way out of it? It wasn't like anyone else would believe that he was waiting for a time-travelling woman to return. Mentioning that would be a sure way to get himself a psychiatric evaluation. Zach realized that he could be in a lot of trouble, indeed.

CHAPTER EIGHTEEN

2172, Ruins of Washington, former District of Columbia, United States

Willow was back on the eroded pitcher's mound in the crumbling stadium. She wasted no time getting back to her speeder which thankfully was as she had left it. Even though she knew that she had plenty of time, she still found herself pushing the vehicle to top speed. She was eager to discuss her idea with Commander Keene and get his opinion.

2172, Time Enforcement Patrol headquarters, New Panama

Willow held her wrist under the scanner that allowed her admittance into the TEP headquarters. She had messaged while traveling to ask for a meeting with their chief of operations. He had given her permission to report to his office as soon as she arrived.

As his office door slid open, the Commander of TEP lifted his eyes from the screens embedded in the surface of the desk before him.

"Randall, what are you doing back? Your mission hasn't been completed. Surely if you needed resources to complete the assignment, you could have messaged and the AIs would have directed you to what you needed," he began.

Willow squared her shoulders and lifted her chin as she said, "Sir, I have come for your advice. The mission has gotten more complicated. I was successful in preventing the original attack on Professor Tyler, but that hasn't solved the problem of the company trying to ruin him and discredit his research. I need more help."

She began pacing as she talked, "Do the AIs have any more information from the dark web that could tell us which company was behind it all? There is an assassin that is trailing after us. He made an attempt on Zach when we went to his apartment to salvage his research after the place was trashed."

Bishop sat back in his chair and followed his agent's movements around his office with his eyes. It was interesting to note that Willow referred to her charge by his first name. It was apparent that she was becoming personally involved in her mission.

Willow continued speaking, "Also, there is a student on the ship. I think that she is probably the one responsible for the attacks on us that occurred while we were on board. She has made allegations of sexual impropriety against Zach. His career at the University as well as his research funding are now in jeopardy. Even if I can keep him alive, his research may never become a reality. I can go back and keep trying, but I feel like I'm two steps behind at every turn." She threw up her hands in frustration as she finished and stood still facing Bishop.

"I can understand that. Because you prevented the attack that killed the professor in the original timeline, the events unfolding now are unpredictable. However, that often happens in our missions. You are used to having to figure out new options. So, what made you decide you needed to come back now?" he pressed.

"Sir, as I said, I need help figuring out what company is behind it all. Maybe we could send another agent to apply pressure on the executives behind hiring these people and get them to cancel the hit on Zach. If we can't do that, I have another idea that I wanted to suggest. It's rather complex, and I thought it would be better to speak in person."

Bishop was curious what she had in mind. Putting pressure on the company behind this mess was a good suggestion. If that move was successful, her other idea might not be necessary. "Alright. You may return to your quarters while I speak with the Archivists to see if we can get any leads on the company involved. We will talk again after they have had some time to sort things out."

Willow knew that she was dismissed and that she shouldn't push anything further at this time. "Thank you, Sir," she replied before turning and leaving.

Back in her quarters, Willow was restless and needed to get rid of her nervous energy while she waited. Grabbing her gear, she headed to the pool. Swimming some laps was the perfect way to settle her mind.

The afternoon passed slowly but, finally, Willow received a summons back to Commander Keene's office. Eagerly, she made the short trip and scanned herself in.

Bishop invited with a wave of a hand in the direction of a chair in front of his desk, "Have a seat, Officer Randall"

When she sat in the designated chair, Bishop continued with a sigh, "The Archivists have had no luck identifying the company behind the attacks on Professor Tyler. So, it's time to hear your other suggestion."

Willow had not been hopeful that the company would be identified. The lead that had alerted them to the fact that there even was a plot against Zach had been a slim one. "Sir, I think that Zach needs to move to a time where his algae idea is more valued."

"The concept was still experimental. Do you think that it actually will work? Our resources are limited, you know, and we can't afford to waste them on something that doesn't produce," Bishop pointed out.

"Yes, Sir. I do think that it will work. I saw the algae on the ship. It was scrubbing the microplastics out of the seawater being pumped into the glass cylinders. It was being done on a very small scale, but it did work and there is potential to ramp up the production so that a meaningful difference could happen quickly."

Bishop nodded. "You know that the Time Tribunal would have to approve the professor's being transported to this time," he reminded her.

"Yes, Sir. That's part of what I wanted to discuss with you. My idea isn't to move him to our time. I think that we would see better results if we moved Zach to a time a few decades earlier. That way, we would already be seeing the benefits by this point in the timeline."

Bishop pondered her words. It wasn't actually a bad idea. He asked, "The professor's cooperation would certainly be necessary. How agreeable do you think he would be to the move? Not everyone can wrap their head around time travel."

Willow broke eye contact with the Commander for a moment and mumbled, "Um, I may have had to tell him that I was from the future to secure his cooperation." Looking back up, she went on, "Zach took it quite well and I don't think that he would be opposed to the move. He wants to see his discovery make a difference and he's frustrated with the personal attacks being raised against him. There hasn't been a final decision made about his position with the University yet, but I expect that another former student needing money will come forward with a second accusation and that will cement the dean's decision."

Bishop nodded. Willow's theory was likely to happen. That is what he would do in the situation. Mulling over Willow's idea, he asked, "What time period were you thinking?"

Willow had considered when she would suggest carefully. It needed to be at a point in time when time travel was a reality to the leaders of the world. Also, if the ocean levels had receded to about their current point, it would be easier to develop the infrastructure that would be needed to support the venture. "I was thinking around 2130?" And then she put forth the rest of the plan, "I was thinking that this Time Tribunal could write a message to the court of that time and you could deliver it in person, Sir. That way, the world leaders would, perhaps, be more willing to put forth the resources Zach would need to get his operation up and running."

Bishop considered Willow's words. It sounded like an idea that might actually work. Still, the professor's algae process was unproven. It would be a gamble, though perhaps not a longshot. He replied, "Given the way you have described the professor's current situation, it would seem that he is unlikely to be allowed to develop his discovery in his present time. Plus, the technology may not survive the coming climate upheavals, should he remain in his own time."

After another moment of consideration, he decided, "Okay, Randall, I will take your idea to the Time Tribunal and let them decide." As another thought occurred to him, Bishop asked, "Is the professor still at the mountain house? Is that location secure?"

Willow replied, "Actually, Sir, since I had already convinced Zach that I was from the future, I saw no reason to leave him unsecured while I travelled to my jump location and back. We travelled to Washington, D.C. together and he is currently at National's stadium awaiting my return jump. He has viable samples of all his algae there with him. Whatever the Tribunal decides, I need to go back so that he isn't found there and prosecuted for trespassing."

Bishop nodded, "Alright then. We have some time to make this decision. I will talk to the Justices of the Court and let you know what they decide."

Relieved that there was a potential solution, Willow recognized that she had been dismissed so she rose and headed back to her quarters. Being able to manipulate time made it all the more difficult for time travelers to wait.

2130, Time Tribunal Courtroom, New Panama

Bishop Keene had made the time jump himself. He didn't often get to travel much in his present role, and he missed it. The judges in his own time had approved Willow's idea and written a letter to the court he was now standing in front of. There was a lively discussion going back and forth between the judges as they talked about the merits of acting on a future Tribunal's recommendation. Such communication from the future was unprecedented.

After the judges in his time had approved his trip back, Bishop had asked Willow to prepare a list of the resources she anticipated that Professor Tyler would need to get his plastic-scrubbing algae into production. He had that with him now, in anticipation that the Court would ask that question. These judges were known for being very conservative regarding time travel and manipulation of the timeline. Bishop listened to the spirited discussion and felt that the final decision could go either way.

2172, Time Enforcement Patrol headquarters, New Panama

Willow had been going stir crazy in her quarters for days waiting to hear what the court in 2130 decided. She had been hopeful when the first hurdle had been navigated in getting the judges of this Tribunal to agree with her plan. She spent a lot of time swimming in the pool. Somehow, it made her feel closer to Zach. She was surprised how much she was missing his company. Although she knew that he was safely waiting for her to come back, she couldn't help the feelings of worry. She logically knew that she would return before anything else could happen and attributed her concern to the many attempts that had been made on Zach's life. She resolutely pushed aside the lonely feelings that washed over her as she lay in bed at night. However, in her dreams, she felt Zach's warm body wrapped around her. When she woke in the dark of night, she tossed and turned as she tried to put those thoughts out of her mind.

It was a relief the next day when Commander Keene called her to his office. She hurried over and scanned in. When she again stood before her boss, he motioned for her to have a seat before he began, "Officer Randall, I've just returned from the Time Court of 2130 and I have their verdict."

Seeing her eager anticipation, he wasted no time telling her, "They have decided to allow Professor Tyler to be transported to their time, along with his algae, for the purpose of establishing a system that will cleanse the oceans of microplastics. He will be given one tanker. It has been suggested that he focus his efforts on the Atlantic first."

He went on, "As you pointed out in your list of necessary materials, there must be a place to receive and process the crude oil that is generated by the algae. They have agreed to reclaiming and refitting a refinery in what used to be Texas. Wind, solar, and tidal energy will be used to process it into usable fuel. The courts in our time are hopeful that we can eventually have enough material to power rockets into space again. Many of the satellites have fallen from orbit or become inoperable. Being able to replace aging equipment was a major selling point for both Time Courts," he concluded.

Willow was thrilled with the news and a broad smile lit her face as she struggled to contain her elation. Bishop assessed her expression with speculation as he directed, "You will return to the professor and transport him and his algae to the year 2130. I have arranged for a TEP agent in that time to escort the two of you to New Panama where you will introduce the professor to the judges of the court. That will complete your mission and you will return here."

At his words, Willow felt a wave of disappointment. She realized that, when she had been coming up with her plan to save Zach, she hadn't envisioned leaving him behind. The only way she would know if his algae did their job would be an alteration in her reality that she might very well take for granted. The notion left her feeling vaguely dissatisfied.

Bishop saw his agent's expression and asked, "Is there a problem, Randall? I thought that you would be happier that your solution is poised to have some very real benefits for the world we live in."

She replied, still trying to sort out her feelings enough to express them, "I am, Sir. It's just that I guess I thought that I would be able to help Zach get his project going." With another thought she suggested, "He is going to be all alone, trying to navigate a new time in a world that is so different than what he's used to. I think that he should have someone help him acclimate."

Bishop reassured her, "I'm sure that the judges will appoint a TEP officer or two to do exactly that."

Willow felt suddenly jealous of those officers and protested, "But they won't know how Zach's system works."

"I'm sure he will be able to explain it to them," Bishop replied. Speculatively, he asked, "Is there some reason that you want to remain in 2130? How long do you think you should stay there?" TEP agents conducted long-term assignments upon occasion. When their mission was finally completed, they returned, having aged while on assignment.

Willow thought about the questions and tried to come up with a reasonable response. While she was still thinking, Bishop asked gently, "Is it possible that you have developed

feelings for the professor? I have never seen you so emotion-
ally invested in an assignment."

Willow was floored by the question. Forced to give
words to the feelings of loneliness and longing for Zach's presence, she realized that was exactly what had happened. After
a stunned moment, she admitted, "Yes, Sir, I think I have." On
the heels of the admission, she blurted out her next thoughts,
"What am I going to do about it?"

Bishop saw the dismay on her face and felt compassion.
He knew that, as her commanding officer, he should tout the
virtue of duty over self. However, that thought always was
accompanied by an unsettled feeling in his own heart. He had
a vague sense of regret although he had no recollection of why
the thought of offering such advice made him feel that way.
Instead, he asked, "If you didn't have a job to do, what would
you want to do about it? What future would you envision for
yourself?"

Immediately, Willow pictured herself on a tanker ship
floating in the middle of the ocean. The deck was littered
with glass tubes of dark green algae and she was working side
by side with Zach as they brought his dream to reality. She
looked steadily at her commanding officer and said, "Sir, I'd
stay with Zach in 2130 and work with him to clean up the
oceans."

Bishop had suspected as much. While there was a lot of
time spent on training agents for time travel, he realized that
people who were distracted in their work made costly mis-
takes. He needed his team to have all their heart in their missions. When there were developments that caused an agent
to focus on other things, he needed to remove them from the
field.

Clearing his throat, Bishop pronounced, "I will have to
get approval from our Tribunal for you to join him. The final

decision will be up to them."

Willow was surprised that Commander Keene wasn't telling her to put her feelings aside and do her job. However, before he could change her mind, she thanked him and left.

Bishop stared at the closed door for a few minutes as he thought about the vague perceptions he had. Somehow, he felt that he had once been in the same position and made the wrong choice. Whenever he thought about the lack of someone to love in his own life, he was overwhelmed with remorse.

CHAPTER NINTEEN

2018, Washington Nationals Stadium, District of Columbia, United States

Willow had jumped back a few minutes before her other self was due to arrive with Zach. She didn't want to risk leaving him alone for long. The Time Court had thought that it would be a good idea for Willow to stay with Zach and help him acclimate to life in his new time period and assist him with developing his research into a functional process. When she got the news, Willow had been thrilled. She was now carrying a time belt for Zach. The belts had an extension that could be wrapped around objects and this was how they would transport the algae. She had made arrangements with Commander Keene for him to jump to 2130 a few weeks after their arrival to collect their time belts.

Now, however, as she went to the dugout opposite the one her other self would soon leave Zach standing in, she had a moment of insecurity. She had had some time to process the feelings she had for Zach. What if he didn't feel the same way, though? What if she had thrown her career away for a shipboard romance? Suddenly, she was questioning herself and her decision.

She felt a physical pain in her head and realized that her other self must have arrived with Zach. She had heard in her training about paradox but never felt the effects of it before personally. Peeking around the edge of the concrete dugout, she saw them climbing down the stairs to the level of the ball field. The headache became sharp. She felt like she was being stabbed behind her eyes with an ice pick as she watched herself trot out to the pitcher's mound. In the instant that her other self disappeared, the headache was gone. Relieved, Willow stepped up onto the warning track and heard the dirt crunch beneath her feet as she made her way back to Zach.

She was suddenly uncertain if Zach would go along with her idea. Still, she was excited to see his face again. Looking around, there was still no sign of security, thankfully.

Zach saw a figure step out of the opposite dugout. The clothes were different, but he recognized Willow's long blonde hair and slim form. Relief washed over him. As he watched her approach, he could see that she was actually wearing what looked like a dark uniform with several symbols on it.

Suddenly a little shy, Willow smiled broadly as she stepped down into the shadows again. She felt like so much had happened for her. She wanted to throw her arms around Zach's neck and pepper his handsome bespectacled face with kisses. Trying to be casual instead, she said, "Told you that you wouldn't have time to miss me."

Zach smiled his relief and replied, "Good thing because I realized that I would be looking pretty stupid here with my buckets full of algae in an empty ballpark. Did you get the answers you were looking for? Is there a way out of this mess?"

Willow nodded. She invited him to have a seat on the bench, "You probably should sit down. I have a few things to explain." When he had done as she had asked, she continued, "I went back to my time, hoping to get more information about the company that hired Mindy and likely her boyfriend. I thought that maybe they could be convinced to leave you alone. However, that avenue was a dead end. There just wasn't enough surviving information after the EMP to narrow it down. I'm sorry," she added.

"Then what am I going to do?" he asked, feeling rather hopeless. "I can't keep running like this and I may not have a job at the University much longer. Without access to their equipment and funding, I won't be able to set up the filtration system I envision."

Willow nodded. "I know. I had an idea that I thought offered an alternative solution and that was the rest of the reason that I went back to talk to my commander. I needed approval before I could tell you about it. I have made arrangements for you to have a tanker ship and you will be able to oversee the development of the glass tubes and filtration system you need to set up your process. Your concept is being put into production," she announced happily, touching her hand to Zach's thigh as she spoke.

Zach's mind was reeling. Her hand on his leg was distracting him. He couldn't believe his ears, "What? How?" he asked. He thought he saw a shadow pass over her face for a moment and she hesitated a fraction before she began speaking again, "Well, that is the tricky part, Zach. What would you say if you could make a real difference? But, just not in this time."

Zach replayed her words in his head before repeating them back aloud, "Make a difference but not in this time? What does that even mean?"

Willow went on to describe what she and Commander Keene had been doing in her absence. She outlined the resources he would be given for the project.

Zach replied, "You want me to time travel and set up my system in another period? What year are you talking about?"

"2130," she replied quietly.

Zach remembered she had said that she was from 2172. "Why can't I just come to your time?"

Willow replied, "Well, if you start a few decades earlier, the oceans in my time could be significantly cleaner."

Zach nodded slowly. The picture was becoming clearer to him. She would move him to a time where he would be safe and then make the quality of her life in 2172 better. Disappointment washed over him. He knew that he should be happy. It really was an excellent solution. He wouldn't have to fear for his life, and he could see his dream become reality. Somehow, though, he wasn't as excited as he knew he should be. He knew that he should be jumping at the chance. However, he would be all alone with only his research. While that had once seemed like a glorious prospect, it now felt empty. Silence stretched between them and he knew that Willow was waiting for an answer. "Um, thank you, Willow. I know that you put a lot of thought into the idea. It's a really good offer."

Willow had thought Zach would be jumping up and down with joy at this point and felt sure that she must have left something important out of her explanation. "I thought you would be happier," she said.

Still sorting out his thoughts, he replied, "I thought I would be too." Zach realized that sharing his thoughts with Willow had become important and he didn't want to give that up, even for his research. Grasping her hand from where it rested on his thigh, he twined his fingers in hers and met her steady gaze, "Willow, is there any way that you would consider staying in 2130 and working on the project with me?"

She smiled but before she could say anything, he went on, "The thought of living my life, in any time, without you being a part of it makes me incredibly sad. I think that I've fallen in love with you."

Willow's smile grew bigger and she threw herself into his arms as she announced, "Oh, Zach, while I was away, I realized I've fallen in love with you too."

Her lips met his in a tender, moving kiss that was a soul-deep melding of emotions. When they finally separated a short time later, Willow spoke again, "I already told my commander that I was resigning from TEP and that I wanted to work with you to make your project a success."

Elated, Zach replied, "Then what do we need to do to get going?"

Willow took a time belt from around her waist and handed it to him. That was when he realized that she had been wearing two of them. "Put this on. Then, we'll have to carry everything out to the pitcher's mound." She pulled a tab and a strap extended out from the belt. "Wrap this around the buckets and your backpack. I'll take the cooler with the samples from your apartment. We already had TEP agents in 2130 check out this jump site and it's safe for us. They will be waiting to take us to New Panama. That's the city where we will outfit the tanker and get everything set up."

Willow could see the excitement and love in Zach's eyes and couldn't resist another quick kiss. "You won't feel anything with the time jump. Your belt is linked to mine and I will control making it happen. Are you ready?"

Zach nodded. He couldn't believe how quickly his circumstances were changing. While he knew that he should be afraid, he felt inexplicably happy as he was confident that Willow would be working alongside him. "Ready," he pronounced firmly.

Picking up the picnic bag, she turned and sprinted toward the mound again. This time, Zach had his buckets in hand and his backback on his shoulder and ran behind Willow to keep up. Atop the small rise, she knelt and drew out her extension and Zach followed suit. He heard a low beep as she pressed a button with her elbow. She leaned over and kissed him again as she pressed another button and the dark shadows of the silent stadium shifted.

EPILOGUE

2130, Atlantic Ocean, off the coast of North America

The flood waters had mostly receded, and the ice caps had reformed as the Earth had taken decades as it tried to heal itself after the light of the exploding star had faded, leaving the planet with only one sun again. Still, the flood waters had washed tons of garbage material from landfills out to sea. An island of garbage had formed in the Atlantic. While it wasn't as large as the one in the Pacific, it still stretched for several miles in diameter.

Zach was standing on the deck of the *Clean up the Sea*, the converted oil tanker that housed row upon row of glass cylinders filled with his algae. The past six months had been a busy time for the couple. At first, the Time Tribunal of 2130 had protested Willow's presence. That had not been in the original agreement Commander Bishop had worked out. Zach had appealed to them that he needed help on the project that

only she would be able to provide. When her boss had arrived
to collect their time belts, Commander Keene had spoken
up on their behalf and, ultimately, the justices had relented.
Bishop had taken the belts and Willow's communicator with
him, making their relocation permanent.

They had fashioned some solar and wind collectors that
gave them some power aboard the vessel. Now, Zach watched
Willow as she was piloted the large boat into position alongside a floating island of plastics. Soon, they would be dropping
anchor and begin putting his hungry algae to work. There
were many days that he still felt it was surreal. At first, he had
been afraid to feel happy. Every morning as he woke up beside
Willow, Zach was thankful for the way that changing times
had changed his life.

THE END

OTHER NOVELS BY KAYCEE GALIVAN

Thank you for reading! If you enjoyed this story, you may want to check out my contemporary romantic suspense series, Cops of Chicago. They are connected books, but each can be read as stand-alone novels.

Duty to Serve – Book 1 – Grant and Bronte's story
Duty to Protect – Book 2 – Luke and Thea's story
Duty to Defend – Book 3 – Mac and Riley's story

In case you missed the other books in the TEP series, please check them out. They are also complete stories that stand alone within the series. The chronological order of the books is a little different than the order that they were released in.

Out of Time – Book 4
When Birds Sing Again – Book 1
Golden Opportunities – Book 2
Shifting the Tides – Book 3

I also have an equestrian-themed contemporary romance series set in Kentucky.

Foster Home – Book 1 - Shelby and Rafe's story

All these books are available on Amazon Kindle Unlimited for those who subscribe to that service. They are also available as ebooks on Amazon as well as a printed option. Please check them out.

WORKS IN PROGRESS

I am presently working on Wyatt and Kyle's story for the Foster series as well as the next TEP story which will be a young adult book. Book 4 of the Chicago series is also progressing, so watch for new releases on my Amazon author page and consider following me to see new additions as soon as they are published.

In case you haven't read it yet, an excerpt from the first book in the Time Enforcement Patrol series, "When Birds Sing Again", is included for you to sample.

One final note: if you enjoyed this book, please consider leaving me a review on Amazon and/or Goodreads. It doesn't have to be anything long. Even just a few words or just leaving a rating will help increase my visibility as a self-published author. It also lets me know that people are liking the stories I'm writing. Thank you and happy reading!

BONUS CONTENT

WHEN BIRDS SING AGAIN

by

KayCee Galivan

PROLOGUE

Winter, 1916, St. Petersburg, Imperial Russia

Zander Blix crouched low and tried to avoid making too much noise as his feet crunched on the gravel surrounding the palatial building he was sneaking out of. He had broken into the Winter Palace of Czar Nicholas II outside St. Petersburg. He was here on a mission to obtain two very specific items that had been deemed culturally or artistically significant. The first item was a complete copy of a Gutenberg Bible. This artifact represented the beginnings of printed books and allowed for expanding education to the masses. They had been printed in the 1450s and the royal House of Russia had one in their possession.

Zander was always impressed by the opulence of palaces like the Czar's. There was golden gilt on the ceiling moldings, and he had been unable to resist taking a moment to appreciate the grandeur of the amber room. The elegance was in remarkable contrast to the conditions in which most of the ruler's subjects lived. Zander was dressed as one of those peasants with coarse woolen trousers and tall boots. He also wore a woolen tunic belted at the waist and a heavy overcoat with a fur-lined hat.

The other item he was sent to procure was a Faberge egg. The master metalsmith had crafted exquisite works, some of which had been lost to history. He knew which eggs to avoid so that he wouldn't impact the timeline. In his search, he had managed to obtain not just one, but two of the priceless artworks. With all of Faberge's other works having been destroyed during the upheaval, the ones in Zander's possession would be the only two examples in the future. Both the Bible and the eggs would be on display in a special exhibit in his time. The remaining population liked to go to see items that were part of their history and art. Zander was a member of the Time Enforcement Patrol, also known as a TEP officer. He was from the year 2170 and in that time, the Earth looked very different.

Once he had secured the items, Zander had slipped out of the palace and made for the train station. He now needed to travel nearly 2,000 kilometers east to Yekaterinburg in order to make his escape. As he sat on a hard bench in one of the train cars, he thought that, perhaps, imperial guards had come galloping into the station just as the train had been pulling out.

Zander worried that the telegraph lines would be faster than his train and that he would be waylaid at his next stop. He decided to climb up on top of the train before it arrived in the station. Thankfully, although there were local police who searched it, they never looked on top. It was winter, after all, and the wind chill on top of the train made it a very cold place to be. His beard, normally worn cropped short, had grown out some over the past few days as he worked on his mission. Thankfully, it helped protect his face a little bit from the windchill.

Once they were underway again, Zander made his way back to the deck of the car he had been hiding atop and slipped inside. He tried not to appear colder than the other passengers although there was little heat inside the train car. There weren't any soldiers or policemen inside, so he took a seat again. He pulled a stale biscuit out of his bag and took a bite. He would be spending approximately the next 24-hours on the train so he tried to get as comfortable as he could.

1916, Yekaterinburg, Imperial Russia

When the train pulled into the station, Zander was tired from being up for over a day. He was covered in ash and dust from the coal-fired engine that pulled the cars along. He had decided to depart the train as it was still slowing, hoping to avoid any soldiers or police who might be at the station looking for him.

While there was always a risk of injury, he let the momentum roll him away from the tracks as he landed. Once he was back on his feet, Zander snuck into a stable not far from the train station and slipped into a stall. He saddled the horse and quietly led it out the back door of the barn. He flung himself up on its back and held his pace to a sedate walk as he worked his way through the narrow, muddy streets toward the outskirts of town. It was still dark out as he was headed to the upper pond to the northeast. It was actually an area where the Iset River naturally widened. His destination was the rugged cliffs of a gorge overlooking the pond where the river fed into it. There had been settlements in this area going back to before the bronze age and the cliffs were a solid stone surface TEP could use for their travels.

The major problem that time jumpers faced was the fact that they changed time but not location. So, if one jumped in a random place, in the past there may have a tree or a building in that location and the jumper risked being trapped in that object. For that reason, certain places had been identified as safe locations that functioned as portals because they had been identified as places in which nothing could grow or be built. Rocky outcroppings like the location Zander was headed to were good choices. TEP also liked to utilize well-known historical landmarks, if the location was existing within the timeline of the jump and still accessible in the future. Then they could risk using things like church steps for their jumps. Zander would have loved to have used The Winter palace itself but it had been consumed by the sands and destroyed in their present so he wouldn't be assured of jumping safely. The AIs always plotted the safest locations for them which was what had forced him to travel all the way from Yekaterinburg and back.

1916, Ural Mountains outside Yekaterinburg, Imperial Russia

Zander crouched low over his horse's neck, urging the animal to greater speed. He could hear the sound of wolf-hounds barking in the distance behind him. Through breaks in the trees, he could see the silhouette of a troika against the white, snowy backdrop as it followed him in the distance, and it was drawing closer. He didn't have too far to go now but he worried that his pursuers may get within firing range and he hoped to avoid that complication.

It was likely that he was being followed by local police because someone had observed him stealing the horse. He doubted that his pursuers were looking for him because of his thefts from the Winter Palace. Still, he didn't want to get caught with the precious items in his possession. If he was, he would likely be shot on the spot without any trial.

The horse's hooves were pounding steadily on the frozen snowy trail and it seemed sure of foot, so Zander nudged it to greater speed with his heels. He didn't have much further to go now. He could glimpse the river through the barren trees to his right as the moonlight shone on it. It was unfortunate that the sky was clear. Because the moon was so bright, every time the path opened up into a clearing, he was visibly exposed to his pursuers.

The trail grew steeper and more rugged as the elevation grew. Zander had to slow the horse to allow it to climb among the rocks. The terrain would slow his pursuers in the troika but not the dogs they had with them. He reached for his belt with one hand as he guided the horse with the other. He made the adjustments necessary to program the equipment for his return jump so that it was ready for the final press or the button the instant he was near the right position.

The horse's hooves were ringing on rock now as they were nearing his goal. They burst out of the trees around an outcropping of stone that formed a cliff overlooking the river rushing over rocks below. Zander pulled his horse up abruptly and glanced over his shoulder. The steeper, narrow path would have forced the men to continue their pursuit on foot, but he was still worried about the dogs. However, the trail behind him was still clear although the sound of the barking dogs was getting much closer.

Zander flung himself off the horse and made sure that his cargo was still secure as he ran toward the center of the barren rock. There, he stood still and pressed the glowing button on his belt. One moment he was there and, the next, he was gone. The borrowed horse was now standing alone, winded on the rocky outcropping where the local police would soon find him and return him to the stable. They would search the woods around the cliffs and, even with the aid of the dogs, no trace of the horse thief would be found.

www.ingramcontent.com/pod-product-compliance
Lightning Source LLC
Chambersburg PA
CBHW061529120726
48001CB00004B/1452